Bellowing Hollers

Matt
Enjoy this journey through
Bellowing Hollers
Dez Tovar

D E Z   T O V A R

PAGE PUBLISHING, INC.
New York, NY

First originally published by Page Publishing, Inc. 2017

ISBN 978-1-64082-484-3 (Paperback)
ISBN 978-1-64082-485-0 (Digital)

Printed in the United States of America

CONTENTS

ACKNOWLEDGMENTS

The author would like to extend her appreciation to the following:

Debbie Ogle
Linda Tovar
Teri Jones
Judy Verheggen—I beat you at Scrabble
Nancy Rogers
Robbi Eck
You know what you did . . .

Words to live by:

It doesn't matter where you go or what you do in ten years, you will be ten years older! Do what you dream!

—Kathy Carter

Visualize it and do it! You will not succeed unless you do!

—Santiago Moran

CHAPTER 1

Steve

"Oh man! What happened to him?" Sarah wailed.

Jessie just stood there, wide-eyed, mouth agape, staring at the mutilated body. She could not speak.

Sarah grabbed Jessie's arm and started shaking her, screaming, "We've got to leave! We've got to get the police! The preacher said for us not to come here! Oh man, shoulda listened . . . man, why didn't we listen?"

Jessie turned to Sarah and said in a very eerie voice, "Shoulda, woulda, coulda died! We're here now! Can't change that! Steve is dead! We can't change that! Let's just get the hell out of here! We'll go back to the church and tell the preacher what happened. He'll tell us what we should do."

"We have to take him!" Sarah said, still staring at the body, which was once Steve.

"We can't take him! We can't! We just need to leave this death camp before something happens to us," Jessie said, grabbing at Sarah, pulling her toward the bus.

Sarah resisted, yelling, "Oh why, God, why?"

Jessie, practically dragging Sarah to the bus, was saying, "We have to go. I can feel them out there watching us. Let's go, Sarah." Finally she shouted, "Sarah, let's go!"

Sarah quit fighting Jessie; they both turned and ran over to the bus. Jessie slid the side door closed while Sarah got in on the passenger side. Sarah quickly slammed and locked the door. She went to the back to lock the sliding door and put the top of the camper down.

Jessie ran to the other side of the bus, opened the driver's door, and slammed it shut. She ran over to the fire and picked up Steve's duffel bag, tossed it over her shoulder, and ran back to the driver's side door of the bus, opened it, and tossed the bag in between the seats. Jessie got in and started the bus.

Sarah screeched, "What in the hell are you doing?" as she locked the last latch into place.

"I got Steve's bag! He won't need it anymore. *We* may need something out of it." Jessie exclaimed. She turned the headlights on. Jessie looked out the windshield toward the woods. She saw something surrounding them, glowing in the dark. It looked to her like little evil red eyes lurking in the blackness, watching every move they made.

Sarah, still in a panic, reached behind Jessie to make sure the door was locked. It wasn't. She locked it, and as she did she noticed the red specks as well. "Oh shit, Jessie, what is that?"

Jessie whispered, "I don't know. I do know that's what killed Steve." As she put the Volkswagen bus in first gear and started rolling forward toward the highway, she said, "I bet Steve fell asleep. Remember what the preacher said? 'Don't sleep at night or you won't ever wake up!'

Sarah answered, "Oh yeah, but I thought he was just messing with us. Oh Jessie, we should have listened. He was just so creepy, though. So tall and big—he was as big as a giant. I bet he was at least six five and creepy!"

"Yeah, but man we shoulda listened. A dude can't help how he looks."

CHAPTER 2

Wrong Way

Jessie looked at Sarah as they started pulling onto the highway. "We go right, right?"

"No, left. Remember, you flipped a bitch when you pulled in? You parked the opposite way, remember?"

Jessie answered, "Yeah, but we're going back to the church, right? We go right, right?"

Sarah, desperate, said, "No! Jessie, go left. We need to go back south, look at your compass! We have to get out of here!"

Jessie looked at her compass. "Oh shit, Sarah. Look at this."

Sarah stood to look at the compass and asked, "Why is it spinning?"

Jessie said, in that eerie voice again, "This is bad, it was working fine earlier. I'm getting really freaked out here. This is not a coincidence, I'm sure of it. Which way should we go? You decide."

Sarah looked at Jessie and said, "If I *am* wrong, you can't blame me!"

"If you're wrong, we may not be alive to point fingers at each other. Which way?" Jessie snapped.

"Go the way you said we should go. Your instincts are usually right. So go right."

Jessie turned right and started slowly down the dark highway. She was thinking, *This is the darkest place I've ever seen.* The road narrowed and seemed to be getting darker.

CHAPTER 3

Dead Steve's Bag

Jessie drove along at 25 mph, her headlights on high beams. It was so dark, she dared not go any faster. Sarah clicked on the overhead light.

Jessie screamed.

Sarah screamed, then yelled, "What?!"

Jessie asked, "Why are you turning the light on?"

Sarah questioned, "Is that why you screamed?"

"Yes," Jessie answered. "You scared me."

Sarah said, "Well, don't do that again. You just about gave me a heart attack!"

"What do you think you did to me?" Jessie answered. "Why are you turning the light on, anyway?"

Sarah said, "I want to write all of this down, just in case well, you know, just in case. I will go to the back if the light bothers you."

Jessie said, "I can't see out the window with the light on. It's the glare, you know? But don't go to the back either. Can you wait to write? Why don't you get the flashlight out of the glovebox and look in that bag to see if Steve had a gun or something?"

Sarah looked at Jessie for a few seconds, then asked, "Why would he have a gun?"

Jessie replied, "He was a shit kicker. Don't you think he would have a gun, or at least some type of weapon?"

"Jessie, do you know what year this is? Just because he's a cowboy doesn't mean he carries a gun," Sarah said disgustingly. "And besides, Steve didn't seem like the gun-slinging type."

"What is the gun-slinging 'type,' Sarah?" Jessie asked sarcastically. "And by the way, in case you forgot, Steve is not any type anymore! They got him!"

"I know!" Sarah snapped. "You know what I mean!"

"Look, I'm sorry," Jessie said. "My nerves are shot. I can't see a thing now, and it's getting foggy."

"Should we stop?" asked Sarah.

"Hell no!" answered Jessie. "I'm going to keep going to the church. It should be here soon. It was only about fifteen miles or so. I'm going to keep going until we get there. You look in the bag to see if he had any type of weapon."

Sarah got the flashlight and started digging around in the bag. She ended up dumping it on the floor of the bus. She picked up a cell phone and said, "One cell phone, dead! Just like the one I brought. Dead because *someone* never had the lighter fixed like she promised."

"I already apologized for not having it fixed! You already forgave me. You can't bring it up again!" Jessie snapped.

Sarah said, "OK, you're right. I shouldn't bring up the fact that you promised you would have this *old bus* fixed up, just like new, before our *big trip*. Shit man, you have tape holding your windshield in."

"OK, this again," Jessie said. "I didn't have time to replace the window seals, so instead of us getting cold, I duct-taped it. Why are you always living in the past? We went through this already! The past is gone. You agreed to come. We're here. It's now! We're both shitting ourselves, let's not turn on each other. We need to stick together!"

"We've gone over twenty miles now, still no church. I'm getting really freaked. Did you find anything else in the bag?"

Sarah held up a horseshoe and a small pocketknife.

Jessie glanced over and said, "All right, you get the good luck, I get the knife," then laughed a phony laugh.

"That's fine with me," Sarah said. "I don't think I can ever stab anything anyway."

Jessie asked, "Not even after you saw what they did to Steve? I'll stab anything or anyone. I won't let them do to us what they did to him."

Sarah handed the knife to Jessie and put the horseshoe in her back pocket.

Just then, Jessie noticed a blur of lights through the fog.

"Look, Sarah! There's the church," Jessie said. "I wish it wasn't so foggy, I can't s—" Just as she wished, the fog cleared. She slammed on her brakes, stopped, and they just looked at each other. At the same time, they said, "Freaky!"

Jessie looked in the rearview mirror. It looked as though it had not been foggy in the least bit. She looked at Sarah and said, "This is getting more weird, man."

It felt like hours since they left the place where they were going to camp. Jessie looked at her watch to see how long it had really been. Her watch had stopped. Not only had it stopped, on the digital face it read "777."

Jessie asked, "Sarah, what time is it?"

Sarah looked at her watch and said, "I guess my battery died, it stopped at 9:48."

"Mine isn't the battery, mine is digital! If it were the battery, the face would be clear, don't you think?" Jessie said.

"I guess it would."

"Today must be our lucky day." Jessie took her watch off and handed it to Sarah.

Sarah took it and said, "That's cool, more good luck. Can I have this good luck too?" She put Jessie's watch in her front pocket.

"We need all the luck we can get," Jessie answered. "Let's get to the church." She put the bus in first gear and started rolling.

CHAPTER 4

Lost

They went a little ways, but slowed when they noticed a sign off to the right. "Do you see that?" Jessie asked.

BELLOWING HOLLERS HELL#
POPULATION ___
WELCOME HOME!
NOW U R HERE U'LL NEVER LEEVE

"Bellowing Hollers Hell?" Sarah said, frantically. "Population left blank. Does that mean zero?"

As Jessie stopped the bus, she calmly said, "The hell should be 'hello.' Someone scratched the 'o' off. Maybe nobody keeps up with the population, so they painted over it. It says 'welcome home.' It sounds friendly to me. Let's go ahead!"

"Don't be so dumb! It says 'BELLOWING HOLLERS!' We went the wrong way! I say we go back! Just turn around and let's go back! The preacher said, 'You folks really don't want to go to the town that lies before you.' Remember? Look what happened to Steve when he went to sleep."

Jessie said sarcastically, "We don't know that he was sleeping!"

"Why didn't he scream then?" Sarah asked sharply. "If he were awake, he would have screamed, right?"

"I don't know why, Sarah," Jessie answered. "Who knows why they didn't get us too."

Sarah said, as she was trying to calm herself down, "We couldn't go to sleep. We were nervous about Steve being there. We were talking about Steve getting us while they were getting him. We never got to sleep, remember?"

"Oh yeah, man, I remember," Jessie said in a shaky voice. "I know you're right. Let's go the other way, it's only about forty miles or so." Jessie looked in her rearview mirror; the fog reappeared instantly. But it was only behind them. "It got foggy again back there," Jessie told Sarah.

"I still think we should turn around and go back," Sarah said.

They looked ahead. They saw lights before them.

The lights appeared to be getting closer.

Jessie had her foot planted firmly on the brake pedal. "This is really weird. It seems like we're moving, but my foot is pressing down hard on the brake." She checked to see if her foot was on the pedal; it *was*.

"What is going on here, Jessie?" Sarah asked.

Jessie answered, "I don't know, but I do know one thing: the road is too narrow to turn this bus around on. We've got to go ahead." She put the bus in first gear and began to roll forward.

"I guess we have no choice then, go ahead, go straight," Sarah said.

Jessie laughed. "How many times do I have to tell you? Never go straight, always go forward."

Sarah answered, "It's the only way to be!" They both laughed nervously. "At least we still have a sense of humor."

As they got close to Bellowing Hollers, it didn't seem as dark. They noticed a cemetery on the right-hand side of the road. They looked at each other and grimaced. The graveyard went on for a mile before another one on the left-hand side started.

"Damn," Jessie said.

"Or 'damned,'" Sarah said.

"Don't say that! The lights are getting brighter, we're almost there," Jessie said.

Sarah said, "Yeah, I know. That's what I'm talking about."

The graveyard on the left side went for three-quarters of a mile, while the right side continued as well. Jessie said, "It must be a pretty good-sized town with two and a half miles of graveyard. Don't you think? It looks pretty full, from what I can see."

Sarah said, "Let's hope so . . ."

CHAPTER 5

Newcomers

Where the graveyard ended, the town began. It was hazy outside. Sarah and Jessie thought it looked like smog, thick smog. Being from Southern California, they were experts on the subject after all. Jessie kept wiping the windshield, thinking it was just fogged up on the inside. She had her windshield wipers on high (as fast as they would go on a 1970 Volkswagen bus, that is). It was very thick outside.

Jessie stopped as they entered the town limits. She pulled in front of a small Five & Dime store, set the emergency brake, and said, "Shall we?"

Sarah said, "Hell yes! I can hardly wait." She laughed.

The town was lit up like it was early evening. They knew it was much later than that; it had to be around 1:00 or 2:00 a.m. They got out and locked the doors. They noticed there was one other car in town, and it was parked at the other end. Sarah shrugged at Jessie and said, "I can't make out what kind of car that is, but maybe it's the police station."

"Let's go into the store to find out for sure," Jessie said.

They walked up to the door, glanced at one another, and opened it. There was a man standing behind the counter. He looked up, with a strange look on his face and said, "Well-bah."

Jessie and Sarah looked at each other, and at the same time said, "Well, hello." They walked inside. A gray cat walked in front of them, rubbing against Sarah's legs. It then walked to the end of the aisle.

The man was staring at them, not saying anything. Jessie turned to see if perhaps he was actually watching something going on outside. He was not. He was so strange looking. Very pale, with brown shoulder-length greased-back hair. He was very tall and skinny. The weird thing was his attire; he wore a black turtleneck (which seemed too warm for the season), black pants, black belt with a silver-cross belt buckle. He also had a silver-cross necklace, earrings, and bracelet.

Finally the man said, "Welcome, newcomers, to my . . . world-bah. What a . . . bummer-bah. I'm really not used to seeing new . . . beings-bah. How can I get you . . . hopping-bah? Or would you prefer to be left alone while you do your . . . shopping? Bah-ha."

"Well, um . . . actually, we're looking for the police station," Sarah said. "Will you tell us where it is, please?"

The man answered, "You know-bah, nice car-bah. I forgot to introduce my . . . self-bah. They call me J.R.-bah."

Jessie said, with a big smile on her face, "Thanks, man, it's a—"

Sarah interrupted, looking at Jessie, then back to J.R., "I don't mean to be rude, but we really must contact the police. Maybe you have a pay phone? I'll call 911."

J.R. laughed his weird "bah-ha-ha" and said, "My dear . . . sweet lady—"

Jessie interrupted, "She's not your dear sweet lady, mister!"

Sarah touched Jessie's shoulder and whispered, "It's OK, calm down."

J.R. said, "As I was saying . . . ladies-bah (he looked at Jessie and smiled). This may sound crazy, we have no . . . need-bah for the police here in this little bitty . . . city-bah. Everybody does exactly as they are . . . supposed to, or . . . well-bah, you know how it is-bah. Hell, we're all just . . . law-abiding citizens, here . . . in B.H.-bah. So have no pity-bah- ha."

They walked down the aisle to get closer to J.R. Jessie said, "Listen mister—"

J.R. interrupted, "Please . . . bah. J.R., they call me J.R., that's all-bah."

"OK, J.R., we need someone. Is there a sheriff or any law-enforcement agency in this city?" Jessie questioned.

"City-bah?" J.R. said.

Sarah grabbed Jessie's arm and said, "Let's just go down to the other end of town where we saw that car."

J.R. interrupted, "Go if you . . . want-bah. That's just the auto . . . shop, no cop. Bah-ha. He is at the bar, not the . . . car-bah. The auto shop never gets much business . . . you see? Usually everybody just walks to where they're . . . going-bah. It beats pushing, pulling, or . . . towing-bah. Town's not that . . . big-bah. In case you haven't . . . noticed-bah."

Sarah said, "Please, J.R., tell us, is there any law here?"

"No-bah," J.R. answered.

Jessie told J.R., "OK, our friend was murdered, and we need to report it."

J.R. said under his breath, "Sleep-bah."

Sarah asked quickly, "What did you say?"

J.R. answered, "Bah. Nothing-bah-ha.

Jessie quipped, "Did you say sleep-bah?"

J.R. answered, "I did-bah. You know, sleep . . . BFD . . . sleep, sleep, sleep, sleep . . ." he was saying over and over. He began to stare past them, the words drifted off as he looked down. He started fumbling with his pen like he was trying to get it to work. He looked up and shot a glance past them, then looked back down and started fumbling with the pen again.

Sarah and Jessie turned to see what he had looked at.

CHAPTER 6

Stuck

There was a man standing behind Sarah and Jessie. He was very short, with greased-back blond hair. He wore beige Dockers, a white tuxedo shirt (buttoned all the way up), and gold crosses. He had cross earrings (one in one ear and three in the other), a necklace, cufflinks, belt buckle, and two rings, one on each hand. He even had a cross on the tip of each boot. He just stood there, tapping his lip with his left hand. His right thumb was hooked through the belt loop, his fingers tapping his hip. He appeared very nervous.

Sarah and Jessie stood there and looked him up and down.

J.R. said, panicky, "We-bah, didn't hear you, even hear you . . . near-bah-ha."

The man smiled and said, "Obviously." Turning back to face the two girls, he said in a feminine voice, "How do you do . . . ladies? My name is York, Daniel York. You may call me Danny-El. I am *the* Overseer."

"P.I.A." J.R. mumbled.

Daniel shot a quick glance at J.R. Sarah looked at J.R. for a couple of seconds.

Jessie said, "We're looking for the police station. We had a friend that—"

Daniel interrupted, "Oh yes, the ranger reported a body had been found outside the town limits. He is investigating it, as we speak. Did you witness it?"

Jessie answered, "No, we were in—"

19

Daniel interrupted again, "But you were with Steve, when it happened?"

"Well," Jessie replied, "We . . . .we were in the bus while he was outside. He had a fire going, and . . . and was going to sleep outside. But, they got him."

Daniel said, "Uh huh, I see. He fell to sleep, outside, and *they* got him. While you girls were inside, *chit-chatting*," sounding more feminine than usual.

Sarah questioned, "You knew Steve's name? How? We have all his belongings in the car."

Daniel answered, "I *am* the Overseer! I oversee . . . *things*!"

Jessie demanded, "Who in the hell are you? Who in the hell are *you* to say we were chit-chatting? Listen, Danny *boy*—"

Daniel cut in, "Oh boy, my apologies. I *assumed* since you are here, you were not sleeping. My name, by the way . . . is pronounced '*Danny-El*.'"

Sarah said, "That is correct." Just then, she spotted a red and white blur running past behind Daniel. It looked about the size of a small child. She heard J.R. whisper, "Featus."

Sarah asked, "When will we talk to the ranger? We didn't see anything. We were in the bus. We couldn't sleep, so we went out-side to roast marshmallows. We were going to ask Steve if he wanted some. He was sleeping on the other side of the fire, and we—"

Daniel, sounding bored, interrupted, "Walked up to him and found his mutilated body."

J.R. mumbled, "Freakin takeout dinner."

Sarah spun around to J.R. and asked, "What did you say?"

J.R. shook his head back and forth and said, "Not a word, quiet as a . . . bird-bah."

Daniel, still standing in that weird way, but now biting his thumbnail, tapping on his chin with his other finger, said, "*Well*, you see, J.R. here *runs* this store . . . and sometimes his *mouth*. But he is a good *man*." Daniel was staring at J.R. J.R. turned away and started playing with the paperwork he had on his counter. Still star-ing at J.R., Daniel said, "You ladies will just hang out, and if—or when—the Ranger needs you, he *will* find you. Just for a couple of days, or so."

Just then, the red and white blur ran back the other way. *For sure it's a child,* Sarah thought.

"Who is that?" Sarah asked.

J.R. mumbled, "Featus."

"There is a restaurant down by the garage. It is not *too* far," Daniel said. "You girls can walk down there. I am sure J.R. will not mind if you leave your car here while you eat. Will you, J.R.?"

J.R. answered, "You never know-bah, which way it will go-bah. It may get busy . . . bah-ha-ha, bah-ha-ha."

Daniel was laughing too.

Sarah and Jessie looked at each other, shaking their heads.

Just then, the kid stood behind Daniel, peeking around his hip. Jessie was thinking, *What a strange-looking child.* Daniel put his hand down in front of the child's face, with his palm facing toward the girls. The child then darted off between the shelving.

Sarah asked, "Is that your child, Daniel?"

Daniel replied, "*No,* I have no children."

J.R. mumbled "Featus" again.

Sarah turned to J.R. and asked, "Why do you keep saying Fetus?"

J.R. snapped, "Why do you keep . . . asking-bah who is that child-bah?"

"Featus," Daniel called as he stepped to one side of the aisle. "Come, let us introduce you to these *beautiful* ladies."

Featus stepped out to the middle of the aisle and grabbed his crotch; he waved with his other hand. He had a very strange grin on his face. His eyes were black, with red surrounding the black irises. His body did not look like a child's, but more like a short man. His face was like a five-year-old boy's.

Practically singing, Daniel said, "May I present to you fine *ladies*, Featus."

Jessie yelled, "Featus? What kind of name—"

Sarah grabbed Jessie's arm as she interrupted, "Hello, Featus. It's a pleasure meeting you."

"Hardly," J.R. mumbled.

Sarah glanced at J.R. She turned and noticed Daniel staring, hard, at J.R. Featus was now trying to push behind Daniel. Daniel had his back against the end-cap. Once again, he put his hand down in front of Featus's face, palm outward. Featus ran off, behind the shelf again.

Jessie said, "You know, I think we'd be better off—"

Cutting Jessie off, Sarah said, "Going to get something to eat! Yes, you're right, Jessie, better off getting something to eat at the restaurant. We'll drive down there."

Featus ran behind the other shelf as Daniel took his strange pose again. Daniel said, "You girls *really* should not drive with a flat tire." Then he began chewing his thumbnail again, tapping his fingers against the side of his face.

"Those are new tires," Jessie said, looking out at her bus. "I didn't have a flat tire when I came in here! Did you do—"

Sarah stopped Jessie and said, "We'll go to the auto shop to get air, after we get something to eat."

J.R. said, "Bah-auto . . . shop-bah. Bick the dick is probably slicked, by . . . now-bah-ha."

Jessie yelled, "What in the-bah are-bah you-bah trying to-bah say? Can you—"

Sarah grabbed Jessie by the shoulder and pointed her toward the door. As Sarah pushed Jessie, she said, "Sorry, Jessie forgot her medication. She gets snappy when she forgets to take them. Did you say Bick from the auto shop, is where?"

J.R. said, "Bah."

As they walked past Daniel, Sarah questioned, "Where? Daniel?" Still pushing Jessie to the door.

Daniel smiled and said, "*Yes*, at the Froth Finder, it is next to the restaurant, it's a bar. You *really* must learn to control that *temper*, Little Miss Taffeta."

As they walked past the aisle where Featus was, they glanced over at him. He was standing with his back toward them. Jessie went by first; as Sarah walked by, Featus turned and grinned at her, a very eerie look on his face. He was holding the cat, stroking it.

Sarah shoved Jessie out the door. As the door closed, J.R. yelled, "Here's a message to send . . . Sarah, put a leash on your . . . friend-bah-ha-ha, bah-ha-ha."

Sarah and Jessie turned to look in the store, not believing what had just happened. Jessie walked around to the driver's side and noticed that the back tire was halfway empty. "Shit," Jessie said. "Let's go ask the auto guy if we can use his air, then get the hell out of here!"

Sarah said, "Let's cool out! You don't need to talk anymore! Let me do the talking from now on." They headed for the bar.

Jessie snapped back, "Those guys are freaks, they're nuts! Bah, what is *bah*? And that freakin' fruitcake with the crosses, shit! What about the short kid man? Shit, Sarah."

"That's what I'm talking about, Jessie. We can see they're freaks, but you don't have to express it to them! Featus? What's that? Did his mom forget to have him?" Sarah said, laughing nervously. They continued walking down the street, toward Froth Finder.

CHAPTER 7

The Mechanic

As they approached the bar, Jessie read out loud, "Filthy Froth Finder, sounds yummy." They walked in, and to their surprise it was nearly packed. It was very well lit. Jessie noticed there were mostly men and just a couple of older women inside. As they walked up to the bartender, they noticed all the tables were glass, with a white powder on half of them. The tables with the white powder on them had glasses filled with short straws.

"What kind of citizens—?" Jessie asked.

Sarah broke in, "I'll do the talking, and you just shut up!"

They got to the bar. Sarah inquired, "Is the auto shop guy here? I believe his name is Butch?"

The bartender said, "Bick, yes, over in the corner. He is kind of smashed."

Sarah said, "Thank you. Oh, is that legal? You know, the white powder, is that cocaine?"

"That was smooth and subtle, Sarah," Jessie said, under her breath.

"Cocaine?" the bartender said. "Legal? No, it's necessary. Would you like to see a menu?"

Sarah answered, "No thank you, we need Bick. Thanks, anyway."

The bartender replied, "Good luck!"

Jessie whispered, "Necessary." She rolled her eyes. "I'm going to the little girl's room." Jessie walked to the restroom. It was stainless steel, totally stainless, even the toilets, with crosses all over the place. She finished in there and went out to where Sarah was.

Sarah approached Bick. He was in bad shape. He looked as though he hadn't been sober in years. His face was swollen; his nose and cheeks were splotched with red. His hair was greased with filth. He smelled awful. It appeared he hadn't changed his clothes in weeks, possibly even months. They were grimy, greasy, and ripped. He looked disgusting—and smelled even worse. Bick grumbled, "Newcomers." He looked up, downed another shot and snorted a line of the powder. He said, "Run like hell, girl. You'd be better off dead."

Sarah, trying to cover her nose discreetly, said, "Bick, we need to use your air compressor at your shop. It will only take a couple minutes of your time."

Bick looked up at them and said, "All I have is time."

Jessie said, "Sir, please, we need your help. My bus has a slow leak on the back tire. We really want to leave here."

Bick said quickly, "If it's not your tire, it will be something else. You girls need to run. My wife and daughter . . ." He drifted off as he said "daughter." Tears filled his eyes. He downed another shot.

Sarah looked into Bick's bloodshot eyes. She pleaded, "Bick, what about your wife and daughter?"

Bick, whining, said, "They're gone now. I'm not much of a man, I couldn't even help my family." He took the wallet from his back pocket and pulled out the pictures of his wife and daughter. He handed them to Sarah. "Hell, I can't even help myself. How could I ever help you girls?"

"Where did they go?" Jessie asked, looking at the pictures Sarah had just handed to her.

Bick replied, "My advice to you . . . is run . . . just get the hell out of here!" Rubbing his face, he looked down, tears running down his cheeks.

"Why did they leave you, Bick? Did they leave you?" Jessie asked, afraid of what his answer might be.

Bick said nothing but continued to rub his face, looking down into his empty shot glass.

Sarah pulled up a chair and sat down. "Would you mind if we put air in the tire ourselves? Just tell us where the air hose is," she pleaded with him, "Please Bick, we want to leave."

Bick, sobbing now, looked up at Sarah and then at Jessie, shaking his head back and forth. "If I could help you, I would. I . . . I just can't."

Jessie began to say, "But Bic—"

Bick interrupted, "There isn't a hose! It's been cut! I can't repair it! I tried! You'd be better off leaving on a flat tire." He was practically yelling. People were looking over at them but not saying anything.

Sarah, gathering her wits about her, said, "Where are we? Is this like hell or what? Come on, Jessie, let's just go find a phone, we don't need this."

Bick was staring into his empty shot glass, shaking his head. He said, in a low voice, "There is no way out."

Jessie pulled a chair up next to Bick and sat, grabbing his arm. "Sir, I don't know what happened to your family, but I am sorry. We're scared, we don't know where we are, and this place is the strangest place I've ever been, and we're from *California*." She laughed, but got no reaction from him, and continued. "We had a guy with us that was killed outside of town limits. We met this weird guy that said he was the overseer, whatever that means, and the little freak, Featus. We're tired and want to leave! You can come with us, if you want. I have my Volkswagen bus in front of J.R.'s store. The tire is only half flat, and I have half a can of Fix-A-Flat. I hate to use it, but if the compressor is broken and nobody else has one in this town? That should get us out of here, don't you think?"

Sarah cut in, "Jessie, let's go call my parents, put the tire stuff in, and leave. If he wants to go, he can meet us out there." She got up, ready to leave.

Bick said, in a weary voice, looking at Sarah, "Honey, you girls don't get it, do you?" Looking at each of them, with hurt in his eyes. "You are not leaving. *They* won't let you."

"Who are *they*?" Jessie interrupted, thinking that sounded paranoid, like something her mother would say.

"Maybe it's not so much 'they,' but this damn town!" Bick explained. "I don't know if my wife and daughter are dead or alive. I can't leave not knowing."

Sarah questioned, "Are you saying they won't let us use the phone? Then we just leave! Nobody in this town will let us use a phone? Let's just go then, Jessie."

Bick looked up from his glass, "You said your friend was murdered?"

"Yeah, man. We didn't have anything to do with that, though," Jessie answered.

Bick said, "The ranger won't let you get too far, you will be better off staying in town. You will live longer, that is. Only God knows what will happen to you if you try to skip town. Your automobile is not fast enough."

Jessie yelled, "What are you saying, we're trapped here because some slaughterer decided to do the deed to our friend?"

Everybody in the bar turned to look at them. Bick yelled out to them, "Mind your business!"

The bartender brought over three shots. He set them in front of Bick and asked, "What's going on, ladies? Can I bring you anything?"

"No!" Jessie snapped.

Sarah asked the bartender, "Is there a phone I can use?"

The bartender informed them, "The phone lines are down. I just tried to call out this very minute. There is a storm coming this way, it must have knocked the lines down. Have you somewhere to stay until it passes?"

Jessie snapped, "We have our bus, we camp out in it."

"I wouldn't recommend that, ladies," replied the bartender.

"That's where we've been staying for the past three weeks," Sarah answered. "What's the difference?"

"J.R. down at the store has a couple of rooms he rents out to all newcomers that are stranded. For your own sake, talk to him. Unless of course you would rather stay with this dirty old man in his little shop of whores!" The bartender laughed until he got back behind the bar.

"Go to J.R.'s for the day, girls. He's a reasonable man, and it will be safer there for you than in your car. Trust me, please trust me on this one," Bick said.

"Let's just depart, Sarah. I don't think there's a storm coming. They're all full of shit!" Jessie was saying when the loud sound of thunder hit.

Bick took Jessie's hand in his gently and said, "Listen to me." He was almost whispering. "It is almost morning. Daytime isn't safe in Bellowing Hollers. Go to J.R.'s, get a room, meet me here tomorrow night by nine. Do not tell anyone you are meeting me again. Just act like you think I'm whacked out. Bring your car to my shop now, I will put it inside and hope nothing will bother it before you get a chance to leave."

"What will bother it?" Jessie asked. "This is too freakish, man."

Bick pleaded with them, "Please, I know what I look like and smell like. I used to be a God-fearing man. Now I just fear living. But I'm too much of a coward to kill myself. You got to believe me. I will try to help you, before . . ." he drifted off.

"Before what?" Sarah asked.

"Before you girls get stuck here too!" Bick answered.

"I can't go to J.R.'s," Jessie told Sarah, "After what I said to him."

Bick said, "I don't know what you said to him, but I do know J.R. is a forgiving man. He is one of the few you can trust. He's just a little bit out there, as we all are in this so-called town."

The thunder roared again.

"Go quickly and get your car to the shop, before the storm really hits," Bick urged.

Jessie and Sarah got up and headed out the door. The lights in the street started dimming. They started walking quickly to the other end of town. They were halfway when it started to rain. They ended up running. By the time they reached the store, all the lights in the town were off, except the store lights, and they could make out a blur where the auto shop was.

Jessie told Sarah, "You go talk to J.R., and I will go take the bus to the shop. I'll be back in a couple of minutes."

"I'll smooth things with J.R. for you," Sarah yelled as she went inside the store.

Jessie got into the driver's seat of her Volkswagen. She looked at the passenger seat and saw a dark bulk on the seat. She got her flashlight and shone it at the bulk. It lit up for a split-second, and then the light went out. It was long enough for her to see what that bulk was. She screamed and jumped from the bus. She ran inside the store frantically.

CHAPTER 8

Dark Sunrise

Sarah was inside talking with J.R., when suddenly the door crashed open and in ran Jessie. She was drenched and looked very pale; it appeared as though she was about to pass out. She was hyperventilating. Sarah went to Jessie, put her arm around her, and tried to calm her. J.R. was standing next to Jessie, ready to catch her if she were to faint.

Sarah said, "You're so pale, what happened Jessie?"

Jessie, jumbling her words at first, said, "Cat . . . your . . . saw, it's your cat, J.R., cat's in the bus. J.R., it's the cat, they did it to your cat, J.R."

J.R. shoved past the girls and ran out to the bus. He tried opening the passenger door. The door was locked. Cupping his hands around his eyes and pressing against the window, he could only make out the dark mass, but knew what it was. He was crying, "My cat, my cat." Jessie unlocked the door and opened it for him. J.R. picked up the dead cat and carried it inside. He was sobbing. "Why, Featus, why did he do it to her? Why?" The cat was mutilated. She had chunks of hair, skin, and meat missing from her body.

Sarah and Jessie followed J.R. inside. The thunder was getting louder, and the rain falling harder now. Jessie said, "I better get the bus down to Bick's shop before the storm gets worse." She turned and walked to the door.

As she opened the door, J.R. stuttered, "S-stop-bah. D-don't go alone-bah! S-Sarah, g-go with her-bah, and r-run back q-quickly-bah. I'll w-wait for you ten m-minutes-bah. I-it's only g-going to g-get worse-bah. I-I h-have a room f-for you-bah. S-she had k-kittens, t-too young to survive-bah." J.R. was standing there, petting the dead cat, as though she were alive.

The thunder was getting louder and the rain pouring down even harder now.

Sarah and Jessie were heading out to their bus. Sarah said as she exited, "We'll help you when we get back. We'll feed the kittens and help you bury your cat."

J.R. answered, "Just hurry back-bah. It's getting closer n-now."

They ran quickly to the bus, as they drove to the other end of town, Jessie told Sarah, "You need to check out the bathroom at the bar. It's really, really bizarre, man. There are silver crosses all over, and the entire room is made of stainless steel. It's wild looking."

Bick was standing at the garage door, waiting for them. Sarah asked, "What kind of crosses?" Bick raised the door as they approached.

As they pulled inside the garage, Jessie answered, "You know how that freak Daniel wore all the gold crosses and J.R. wore all the silver crosses? Well, it was like that, only they were all made out of silver metal stuff and in the bathroom. Just a bit weird, you'll see if you go in there tomorrow." Bick lowered the garage door as Sarah was getting out. Jessie stayed in the bus and got some things together to take to J.R.'s.

"I don't want to go in there, I want to leave first thing," Sarah said, then closed her door.

"Bick, is that your car over there?" Sarah asked about the car in the other bay.

"It's not mine, mine's out front," Bick answered. "You girls need to get going!" He was looking out the window. Sarah glanced out and hurried to the bus.

Sarah slid the door open and got her backpack. "Let's go, Jessie. It's getting strange out there. There are people running all over the place."

Jessie handed Sarah a few things. "Can you put this in your backpack? Here's your jacket." Jessie got out of the bus and put her jacket on. The thunder was louder than ever now, and the rain sounded like a rushing river. The lights in the shop went out for a couple of seconds, then came back on.

Bick yelled over the rain, "Girls, go now! See you tonight, around nine."

"Hold on, I need to lock the doors!" Jessie called back.

"It won't do any good! They have a slim-jim! They can unlock anything."

Sarah and Jessie took off out the door. There were fewer people running about. They were drenched as soon as they exited the shop. They ran to the other end of town. It was very dark, almost pitch-black outside. Sarah noticed what appeared to be the sunrise beyond the pouring rain. It was like an underlying brightness, you really couldn't see it, but it was more of a sensation. She put that out of her mind when they reached the store.

J.R.'s store light seemed to be the only light on in town. Jessie opened the door. They walked inside. J.R. locked the door behind them. "Come on back . . . here-bah, to my shack-bah. I live . . . more like behind the . . . store-bah. It's attached-bah, so not to fret-bah. You won't get attacked-bah, or wet-bah-ha-ha-ha, bah-ha-ha."

They walked through the first door. J.R. stopped and locked the doorknob, two deadbolts, then put a two-by-six-inch board across the door in brackets. They walked through the little walkway past the second door. J.R. had four deadbolts and three two-by-six boards to put in the brackets made for them. He locked it all, placed the boards in the slots, and turned to them and said, "It's tearful to be so . . . fearful-bah. We must be aware and take . . . care-bah."

Jessie questioned, "I thought you said there were only law-abiding citizens here in Bellowing Hollers?"

"There are," J.R. mumbled, "But I said B.H."

"Riiiiiiight," Jessie said, sarcastically, shaking her head and peering at him out of the corner of her eyes.

Sarah tapped Jessie's shoulder and gave her a Mother, behave look. Jessie said, "OK, I forgot."

Sarah said to J.R., "Thanks for renting us a room. Bick said you would."

"Bah, yeah-bah," J.R. answered.

"He also said something that kind of bothered me," Sarah continued.

"He only said one-bah-thing-bah that brought you pain? Bah-ha-ha." J.R. laughed.

Sarah laughed, "Well, not only *one* thing, but one thing in particular."

J.R. asked, "Bah-what?"

"Bick called us *newcomers*; you called us newcomers when we first got here. Why do you say we're *newcomers* instead of strangers, guests, out-of-towners, or even visitors?" Sarah asked.

J.R. replied, "Well-bah, that's just what we say-bah. Is that OK-bah? No BFD-bah."

The thunder started up again, shaking the house, growing louder.

CHAPTER 9

Locked Down

J.R. yelled over the thunder, "I am very tired-bah, you look pretty . . . wired-bah. You go to sleep-bah, you won't hear a peep from me . . . until seven thirtyish-bah. All questions will wait . . . until eight-bah. Don't go out . . . side or you will be in for a ride-bah. Good night . . . sleep tight-bah."

Sarah yelled back to J.R., "We have questions. We want to leave. We need a phone. Do you have a phone we can use? Please at least answer our questions."

J.R. yawned, then said, "Very . . . sleepy-bah, it's really getting creepy-bah. I'll show you girls to your . . . rooms-bah. It may need a . . . broom-bah." Then he mumbled, "I'm helping you bah ha aren't I bahaha ba?"

Just then the thunder hit. Sarah grabbed Jessie's arm and said, "We just need one room, J.R." The lights dimmed for a few seconds.

J.R., squinting his eyes, looking from one to the other, said, "I see. Bah-ha-ha, bah-ha-ha."

Jessie snapped back, "It's not like that, J.R! Don't assume. We're just scared right now!"

J.R. mumbled as he walked down the hall, "Sniippy, don't forget your pills . . . bah-ha-ha." He pushed the bedroom door open and pointed. "Good . . . day-bah ladies, see you when it's . . . shady-bah."

Sarah fumbled in the dark for the light switch. She found it, turned it on. Nothing. The light did not come on. She was going to call J.R. when the hall light went off. She heard the door slam closed

34

and the sound of a lock, and then another. "He's paranoid. I just heard two locks click after he closed his door," Sarah said to Jessie. She started feeling around on the dresser top for light of some sort.

Jessie struck a match and asked, "Are there locks on this door?" Jessie found a candle on the dresser and lit it. Sarah found a candle and lit it off the one Jessie was holding. They found a few more and lit them as well. The walls were shaking from the thunder. The bedroom seemed very clean. They lay back on the bed at the same time. "I'm leaving when we wake up. I hate this place," Jessie told Sarah.

"I'm with you. I am totally freaked out," Sarah said.

The thunder stopped for a few minutes. Sarah heard little crying sounds. "Do you hear that, Jessie?" They each grabbed a candle and began looking where the sound was coming from. They found it. There were three little kittens snuggled up in the bottom drawer of the dresser. Wrapped in a soft cotton cloth. Next to the little box the kittens were in was a container of milk. "I guess we feed the babies," Sarah said, picking up two of the kittens. "You get the last one, Jessie." Sarah went and sat on the bed to feed the kittens. "I wonder where he buried the mother?"

Jessie said, "I'll ask J.R. tomorrow." She put the kitten she was holding down to eat with the other ones.

Sarah snapped quickly, "No! You won't even talk to him! Every time you do, you get all frustrated and start acting the bitch!"

"Look at that kitten I just put down, it looks like Yoda, a gray calico Yoda." Jessie started laughing, which caused Sarah to laugh. "I'll try not to be *acting the bitch*."

The thunder started growing fiercer than before.

The laughing fit stopped when the roar sounded. "Let's sleep. We have so many questions," Sarah was saying. "I'm not too sure I really want the answers."

"I know, I don't want to know. This place is possessed," Jessie was saying. "By what, I'm not sure. Let's just get out of here. The sooner we leave, the better." Jessie took her shoes off and lay back on the bed. She had the kitten lying on her chest.

Sarah put the two kittens back in the drawer. She took her shoes off and sat on the bed. "Goodnight, Jessie."

CHAPTER 10

The Letter

It was extremely warm in the room where Sarah and Jessie were staying. Right when Jessie put her head on the pillow, she went fast to sleep. She began to dream.

Sarah, on the other hand, was not in the mood to sleep. It was too hot, and the thunder was way too loud. She took a pen and notepad from her backpack. She started scribbling:

> *"Where are we? Why are we here? Why can't we find a phone to use? Are we trapped here? Who messed with our bus? Where are the police in this town? Where is the Ranger? Who is the Ranger?"*

Sarah turned that page back and started a letter to her parents. The letter read:

> *"Dear Mother and Daddy,*
>
> *I am writing this letter to let you know what happened yesterday. We may get arrested. We are leaving here tonight and probably will be home before you even get this letter. Let me explain everything from the beginning.*
>
> *Yesterday we picked up a hitchhiker. Before you get mad, let me explain to you what happened.*

Please! It is not Jessie's fault. We were driving on Highway 508 in Washington State, going north. We saw this man carrying a duffel bag and a saddle. We felt bad because everything looked so heavy, but we weren't going to stop. After we passed him, we had a blowout, which is weird because there are all new tires on the car. He was about a half-mile back. We unbolted the tire from the front of the bus. When we put the jack under the car, we couldn't jack it up because the jack was too short. By then, the hitchhiker was upon us. He asked if we would like some help. Jessie, of course, said "no," and that we had it under control. The guy's name was Steve. Steve put his stuff down and went and picked up a piece of wood. He handed it to Jessie and told her to try it. Jessie put the log under the jack. Steve said for her to put the jack on the ground and the log on top; that it would be sturdy that way. Jessie told him she was still not giving him a ride. He said he didn't want one; that he was on his way home, and he was almost there. Jessie told him he should get going then. He said, "Yes, ma'am" and walked off. She lifted the bus with the jack, but it slipped and she smashed her hand. She yelled out. Steve turned back around and told her he didn't want a ride, but likes to help at least one person a day, and he was three behind, so would she help him out by letting him help her. Jessie started to brush him off, but I told her to let him help because it would help him too. She agreed.

See Mother, do not blame Jessie like you always do. She tried to get rid of him. After he finished changing the tire, it was I who asked Jessie to give him a ride. He was a nice guy and was on his way home to Canada. His truck had broken down, and he left it because he didn't have any money to get it fixed. It was the engine that blew up. Anyway, we went a few miles, and there was this road. The sign read "bypass," and it forked off, well we took it. We all agreed that it would get us to Interstate 90. It was beautiful scenery, and everything seemed to be all right. We came upon this church. It was a clean-looking church, but it was weird. We hadn't passed a house, and there were no houses around the church. It was in the middle of nowhere. There was a sign on the church that read, "To Turn You Around Church." There was a picnic area, so that is where we stopped to have lunch. The preacher came out to greet us. We asked him to join us, and he did. He introduced himself as "Preacher." When I asked him why his church was named "To Turn You Around," he answered, "This is where you turn around." Jessie told him we were taking a shortcut and it is too far back the other way. Preacher said there is no shortcut, and Jessie told him it is on the map. That's when it got weird. The Preacher said, "You folks really don't want to go to the town that lies before you." It was strange, but we thought he was just talking. We didn't listen. He also said for us not to sleep at night; that's the main reason we thought he was a freak and just trying to scare us. We were wrong!

We continued on and the sun started going down, so we decided to set up camp. We found a campsite. It was only about 15 miles from the church. We gathered some firewood; Steve said he would sleep out by the fire. Jessie and I were going to sleep in the bus. We couldn't sleep, so we went outside. That is when we found Steve. He was dead. It looked like something had bitten him all over. We left to go back to the church, but we went the wrong way. We ended up in Bellowing Hollers. It's not a very good place. We are scared! You see, they want us to stay, in case the Ranger wants to talk to us. We are leaving anyway. We may get arrested, but we need to leave this bizarre place. I will tell you more when I am able to call or get home. I am so sorry about this, Mother. If we do get arrested, please let Daddy get Jessie out of jail too. Jessie's sister really doesn't have any money to get her out. This is not Jessie's fault. I am the one who wanted to come with her this summer before I go off to college. When we leave here, I am sure we will be heading right back to California, home. I love you both very much."

Love,
Sarah

p.s. Maybe this is all a bad dream!!!!!!!!!!

CHAPTER 11

Terror Dream

Sarah heard the kittens crying. She folded the letter and placed it in the envelope, labeled it, ready to mail. She took the kitten off Jessie's chest and put it on the floor with the other two and fed them.

The kittens were eating when Jessie started swinging her arms, yelling, "No, stop! Get away! Help me, Please help!" Jessie was perspiring badly. Her hair was dripping with sweat. She was screaming, "Get them off! They're eating me." She was sobbing.

Sarah grabbed Jessie's arm and shook her. "Wake up, Jessie. It's a dream. It was a dream."

Jessie stopped yelling and screaming. She was shaking, with her arms wrapped around herself. "It wasn't a dream, it was a terror. It was real! It wasn't a dream! I'm so scared. I never want to sleep again. Let's get out of here, now!"

"What was the dream, Jessie?"

"It was horrible, I can't even begin to tell you."

"What was it?" Sarah insisted.

Jessie was shaking. "It was bad, man. I was sleeping, and these black furry things started crawling all over me. They were eating me alive! I couldn't scream. At first it kind of felt good. It was kind of like I was getting a massage or something. And then I started going numb, but I could still feel them going inside me. They were burrowing inside of me. I could feel them drinking my blood! Oh Sarah, it was so real!"

"No!" Sarah exclaimed.

"Yes! Sarah, that's what happened! It happened to Steve! That's what killed him! And they are living inside of him! They live inside until they find another host!"

"It was a dream, Jessie! That's all, a dream! We don't know what happened to Steve!" Sarah insisted.

"No. Well, yes, I know, but it was real too! You don't understand."

"I do understand, I understand we've got to leave this place," Sarah said.

Jessie pleaded, "Let's go! Let's get our stuff and the kittens and get out of this hellhole!"

They closed up their bag and found a little box for the kittens. They each grabbed a candle to light up their way out. Sarah grabbed the kittens. Jessie took the backpack. They quietly opened the bedroom door. They went down the hall toward the store. The lock was off the door. Just then they heard a train whistle. They glanced at each other, not saying a word, and opened the door that led into the store.

CHAPTER 12

LLL

J.R. was in the store, pulling up the blinds. It was dark, very dark outside. Which made the lights in the store appear very bright. The storm had stopped.

"J.R.," Sarah said.

"Bah!" J.R. answered, "You startled me-bah. Let it . . . be-bah-ha."

Jessie turned to J.R., "We didn't even hear you get up, man. Why didn't you wake us?"

J.R. answered, "Bah-you know, sleep is a precious . . . commodity-bah, and quite an oddity around . . . here-bah. You'll see my . . . dear-bah, uh Jessie-bah."

"No, we won't!" Jessie snapped.

"Well-bah, Hell-bah," J.R. said and turned to flip the "open" sign on.

Sarah grabbed Jessie's arm and told her to cool it.

J.R. interrupted, "Yeah-bah, P.M.S. or . . . B.D.S."

Jessie started to say something, and then closed her mouth.

Sarah asked, "What time is it, J.R.?"

"Time to rhyme and get a watch-bah-ha-ha." J.R. was laughing hysterically.

Sarah said, "Well, J.R., we had watches, but for some strange reason, both of them broke. Is it eight yet?"

"Is there a post office or mailbox around?" Sarah asked. "I need to mail this letter to my parents."

"Oh yeah-bah, me too-bah. I send mail and nobody ever writes me-bah, not even from jail-bah."

"Do you have a phone?"

"I don't have anyone to call-bah, at all-bah."

"J.R.," Sarah said, trying to stay calm.

J.R. interrupted, mumbling, and said, "Sometimes Triple L is the correct thing to do."

Jessie snapped, "Triple L? What? Why don't you ever make sense?"

Sarah, very frustrated now, demanded, "I need to get some answers. If you don't have them, *please* tell me who would know! I need a phone! Who would have one?"

Just then, J.R. started tapping his pencil on the counter and repeating, "Phone, phone, phone . . ." He was glancing down the aisle, then back to his pencil.

Sarah looked down the aisle where J.R. kept glancing. There stood Daniel. She fell silent.

Breaking the uneasy silence, J.R. said, "We didn't hear you come in-bah."

"Of course not, do you ever?" Daniel said, mockingly. He looked over toward Sarah, "Please continue, *Little Miss*."

J.R. mumbled, "L L L, 'Look, Listen, Learn.'"

Sarah glanced at J.R. quickly.

The short boy man, Featus, came out from behind the aisle and stood behind Daniel. He was peeking around his hip. Daniel put his hand in front of his face as he had done the night before, palm out. Featus ran back behind the aisle.

Sarah wondered to herself, *Did Featus get taller?*

Hunger

Jessie remembered what Featus had done to the kittens' mother. Nonchalantly, Jessie took the box from Sarah, which held the kittens, and slid it behind the counter.

Sarah said, "OK, then."

J.R. looked down, shaking his head, rapidly.

Sarah continued, "Tell me this, how many people live here in Bellowing Hollers? Why is the graveyard so big for such a small town? And not even one cop, only a ranger we never see!"

Daniel was staring at her with a disgusted look on his face.

J.R. blurted out, "Bah, let me tell you-bah-ha, there are more dead people living here-bah than live people dying-bah-ha-ha-ha, bah-ha-ha."

Daniel was laughing hysterically at J.R.'s answer. In his hysteria, he managed to say, "There you have it!"

Featus was peeking out from behind the aisle, with a freaky grin on his face. His eyes were glowing red.

Sarah looked at Jessie and said, sarcastically, "Well, shit Jessie, that's exactly what you were saying earlier! Let's go get something to eat. Is the restaurant open? Or does it open at midnight?"

Daniel said in a high-pitched voice, "Oh my, oh my, are they both on the medication that turns them into *bitches* if they forget to take it?"

Jessie blurted out, "Listen to me, you little bitch!"

Sarah yelled over Jessie, "Where is the ranger, Daniel?"

J.R. interjected, "It only gets . . . stranger-bah, when you meet the . . . Ranger-bah."

Daniel, smiling his no-teeth smile, still tapping his fingers on his chin, smirked, "In due time, girls . . . or should I say *ladies*."

Featus came running toward J.R. and Jessie, then stopped ten feet in front of them. His voice sounded like a spoiled child squealing, "I want to feed!"

The four of them just looked at Featus in dismay.

"What the—?" Jessie questioned.

J.R. was mumbling, "LLL . . . LLL . . . LLL . . ."

Daniel said, "Ladies, why don't you just enjoy your stay while you're here in our sweet little town?"

Featus walked past J.R. and Jessie to the counter, where Jessie had slid the box of kittens. J.R. pulled a rather large silver cross from behind the shelf and held it in front of Featus. Daniel could not see what was going on behind the counter. Featus turned and ran back behind Daniel.

Sarah turned to Jessie and said, "Let's go get something to eat. That's why we're so moody, we're hungry!"

Just then, Featus jumped out in the middle of the aisle. He was shaking all over, face red with anger. In his high-pitched squeal or screech, he demanded, "I want to feed!" His eyes were glowing a deep dark red, and his teeth appeared more pointed than usual.

Everybody just looked at Featus in astonishment. This outburst brought shock, even to Daniel. Daniel turned and walked toward the door. Featus followed, looking back with the same look on his face he had the night before when he was holding the mother cat. After the door closed, Daniel and Featus turned right, walking toward the graveyard.

The trio were looking at one another and now remembering to breathe.

Jessie spoke up, "What was all that?"

J.R. said, "That was a . . . first-bah. And I hope the . . . worst-bah."

Sarah questioned, "First what? Hey, did it look like Featus had gotten taller to you guys?"

J.R. answered, "And a close . . . call-bah. He always grows . . . tall-bah. That's all-bah-ha."

Jessie agreed, "Oh yeah, close call."

Sarah said, "And, J.R . . ."

J.R. interrupted, "Featus never . . . talks-bah. He barely . . . walks-bah."

Jessie asked, "How did Featus know about the kittens?"

J.R. whispered, "You girls . . . need-bah, to go blow-bah, ASAP-bah."

Sarah whispered back, "What do you think we're trying to do?"

J.R. in a desperate whisper, "Take me?"

Jessie said, "Let's go."

J.R. said, "It takes a little more . . . planning-bah. Bick will help you with . . . the scamming-bah. Please keep me . . . posted or I may get . . . toasted-bah. I do want to go go go go go . . ." he drifted off.

Jessie looked back at the window, and there were Daniel and Featus staring in the window.

Jessie spoke up, "Go and eat, yes. We're going, now!"

Sarah caught on quickly and said, "Yeah, J.R., can we bring you back something?"

"Yeah, bah," J.R. answered quickly, "Two all-beef patties, special sauce, pickles, lettuce, tomato, on a whole wheat bun. No thanks-bah, just pulling some pranks, bah-ha-ha, bah-ha."

They turned to leave, Daniel and Featus were gone now. "See ya," Sarah said as they walked down the aisle. "Don't forget to feed the kittens, J.R. We'll let you know what's up." They headed for the door.

"Stay close to each . . . other-bah, or you may not see one . . . another-bah, again-bah." J.R. yelled before the door closed.

CHAPTER 14

Grease Trap

As they were walking toward the restaurant, Sarah saw the post office across the street. They walked over to it. It was dark inside, but there was a mailbox outside. Sarah read the pickup times. It read 12:00 noon and 6:00 p.m.

"I wonder if—" Sarah started to say.

Jessie cut Sarah's sentence off, "Just drop it in and don't think of it anymore."

Sarah did what she said. They walked back across the street. "When we go back to the bus, I'll get my cell and plug in to see if it works here. At least I can charge it up here."

Jessie said, "I want to write my mother too. Even though she's nuts, she's still my mother. I'll write my sister too."

"Remember what your mom said when we visited her in Bakersfield?" Sarah asked.

"Don't listen to her, she's psycho!" Jessie snapped.

"You can write at the restaurant if you want. We can mail it on the way back. I have paper, envelopes, and stamps."

"Cool," Jessie said. "Look at Bick washing his car."

"He'll meet us when he's done." She read the sign on the restaurant:

GREASE TRAP
Open from
8 p.m. to 2 a.m.

They tried not to think about the name too much—they were hungry!

Sarah asked where the restroom was. The waitress shook her head and said, "Newcomers . . . go next door to the Froth."

Jessie shot back at her, "We'll be back. Going to the Filthy Froth for freaky pisser." They laughed on their way out of there.

As they were walking next door, Sarah found a four-leaf clover made of wire. She picked it up and said, "Look what I found, more good luck."

Jessie responded, "Oh yeah, as if our Triple 7's and horseshoe have helped us this far."

Sarah said, "Just maybe if we didn't have them, things would be worse!"

"Perhaps."

They entered the bar and walked directly to the restroom. Jessie noticed everybody was staring, and some people were whispering and shaking their heads. Jessie said loudly, "What?"

Sarah kept walking as she put the clover on her necklace. They got to the restroom and opened the door. There was an elderly woman washing her hands. Sarah and Jessie said "hello" at the same time. The lady said "hi," then put her finger to her lip, as if to shush them. She dried her hands then wrote something on a napkin from the bar. She handed it to Jessie.

Jessie read it: *"You girls must leave."*

Jessie started to speak; the lady quickly put her finger up to Jessie's lip and handed her the pen. Jessie wrote as the lady lit a cigarette. She handed it to the lady.

"We're trying to, we're going tonight."

Jessie read: *"Send back help, if you escape alive."*

"We will. What's going on here?"

The lady read it, walked over to the toilet, lit the napkin on fire, and flushed it. As she headed out, she handed them each a silver cross. "You girls may need a bit of religion."

"Thank you, ma'am," Jessie said.

"Keep them within reach at all times. You never know when you might need to pray." The lady walked out.

Jessie and Sarah did not speak while they were in the restroom. They walked back out and heard the bartender yell after them. "See you girls later this evening." Jessie waved at him as the door finished closing.

As they walked back to the Grease Trap, Sarah said, "I see what you mean about the restroom, it's strange!" They went inside and sat at the table next to the window. Bick was washing his windows. There were a few people in the restaurant. They were looking and whispering to one another, just like in the bar. The waitress approached them with two glasses of water and two cups of coffee.

"We didn't order coffee," Sarah told her.

"Everybody gets a coffee, on the house. A lot of folks need coffee to keep them awake, you know?"

"Well, thank you. We need menus," Sarah said.

"Our special this evening is French dip with chips and a pickle" the waitress told them, then stood there.

"OK, can we look at a menu, please?" Sarah requested again.

"That's all we have."

Jessie laughed. "No shit! Well hell, I think I might have the special then. What about you, Sarah?"

"I think I'll have the French dip and chips," Sarah chuckled.

The waitress smiled and said, "Don't forget the pickle." She walked to the back.

Sarah was shaking her head, laughing along with Jessie. They were laughing so hard they didn't see Bick come in. He walked over to the counter to sit down. Jessie yelled out, "Hey, old man, come buy us dinner." She scooted over and patted the seat. Before he got over there, Sarah jumped over to the other side to sit next to Jessie. They put both cups of coffee in front of him. He muttered, "Thanks."

CHAPTER 15

Auto Shop

Jessie asked Bick, "So that's your car, eh?"

"Yes. It *was* my car."

"Well, if it *was* your car, then why were you washing it?"

"It's my job. The ranger says it must be washed weekly." Bick whispered, "That's the car my wife and daughter tried to escape in."

"What? You said 'escape,' Bick. What happened?" Sarah asked.

"We'll talk later about that."

The waitress brought their dinner/breakfast to them. She also served Bick his. As she handed Bick his, she asked, "You're not *lying* to these girls, are *you?*"

"No," Bick said, shaking his head. "Put the ladies' meals on my tab, please, Sheryl?"

"Sure, whatever you say, *shop boy.*" She turned, walking away, laughing.

Jessie said loudly, "What in the heck's wrong with people here, man?"

"She means no harm," muttered Bick.

Sarah asked, "Does that car run, Bick?"

Shaking his head, "No, somebody put sugar in the gas tank and pulled all the wires. It was towed and placed there. They said they found it two miles past the cemetery . . . *abandoned* . . . I had to clean it! Eat up, girls. If you want me to go into details, I'll do it outside." He whispered, "Sometimes I feel like these walls have ears."

They ate quickly and quietly, thanked Sheryl, and walked slowly toward the shop.

"Do tell," Jessie said.

"My wife and I got into an argument about leaving here. She feared this town. They offered me a job running the '*so-called auto shop*' . . ."

"Who is 'they?'" Sara interrupted.

"The ranger and the overseer . . . anyway, she and my daughter took off. See, she had done that before, so I wasn't too concerned at first. She leaves for a couple of hours, and then comes home. Well, you see, this time . . ." He paused, wiping his tears from his face. "She didn't return! The ranger brought the car the next day during one of those freak day storms. He dropped it where it sits now. I believe I was too drunk to see what she saw. When we moved to this . . . town, she did not want to stay here. I thought it would be a nice, quiet place to raise our daughter. I didn't realize how evil it was . . . is . . . until my family was gone."

"How long did you live here before your family disappeared?" Sarah asked.

Bick looked at her, still sobbing and wiping tears off his face. "You believe me, then?"

"Yes, I do!" Sarah said.

"And so do I!" confirmed Jessie.

"We only lived here three weeks before . . . well, my wife would ask, "why isn't there any cars beside the junk cars out back and the ranger's". And ours, of course. Like I said, I was just too smashed to see it. When he brought the car back, it didn't start. I noticed the gas cap was missing, so I looked closer and saw sugar crystals around the opening. So I had to drain it and change out the gas. That's when I noticed the locks on the gas pumps. Reality hit me at that point. I checked under the hood . . . there were no plug wires—or any wires for that matter, all pulled out. No belts, no battery. There was mud all over the outside of the car, even inside the engine where the oil cap was missing." Bick was wiping the tears from his eyes and cheeks.

"So there is no way to fix your car?" Jessie asked.

"No! And that sick bastard! Made me! Clean the blood from the steering wheel! My . . . my wife, my daughter!" Bick was crying. "She must have hit her head! My wife . . . there were these . . . these bl-black fuzzy looking things . . . I . . . I can't, don't know what they are or were. I dream of eyes . . . I saw . . . Anyway, I got the job of cleaning that car and keeping the station." Bick was crying harder now.

"We need to get the hell out of here! I mean now!" Jessie urged and began walking toward the shop. "Let's go!"

Sarah was shadowing Jessie.

"Well, hold on girls," Bick said.

"No!" Sarah said, "You can come with us if you want, otherwise we'll send help back for you."

"Wait!" Bick yelled.

"No!" Jessie yelled back, "We shouldn't have even waited this long! Let's go, Sarah." They started walking faster to the shop.

Bick roared, "I drained the gas!"

They stopped, turned and stared at Bick. "What?" Jessie exploded.

"You girls don't seem to understand! Before I slept, I had to drain it, so it appeared you didn't have any and maybe they wouldn't do anything else to your car."

"You little shithead! How dare you . . ." Jessie said.

"Wait, Jessie," Sarah interrupted, "Can you put it back in now?"

Bick answered, "Yes, I can . . ."

"Great!" Sarah said.

"Not so great, you have other problems."

"What?" Jessie demanded.

"They trashed your VW inside and knocked out the windshield—halfway out, anyway. It's cracked and they bashed in your headlights . . ."

Jessie turned and ran to her Volkswagen.

CHAPTER 16

Trashed Out

Jessie was standing there, staring at her car, when Sarah and Bick ran up to her. She was yelling, "Why? Who the hell did this? Why me, my car!" It looked as though somebody bashed in the windshield with a baseball bat. (Or something equivalent to that.) The headlights were smashed. It looked as though somebody went around the whole bus, kicking it in. They unscrewed the taillights, and somebody had taken both of the red lenses. They smashed the bulbs. The tire was completely flat now.

Sarah went inside to retrieve her cell phone. Whoever destroyed the outside also wrecked the inside. She started digging through the rubble. There were fuzzy black balls mixed in with their belongings. She had a stick she would push them out of the way with. "Bick, what are these things?" She continued looking for her phone.

"Those are the things that were in my car too." Bick was just standing there, hands in pockets, looking to the ground.

"They took my phone! Jessie, I can't find the flat-tire-fix stuff. Where is it?"

Jessie opened the back hatch and started throwing the garbage out on the garage floor. She had a piece of cardboard to knock the black things out with. "What's going on, Bick? Who did this, man?"

"That's what I've been trying to tell you girls. They won't let you leave."

Sarah turned to Bick, tears in her eyes. "Why not, Bick? We didn't do anything."

Bick said, in a low voice, "Come out here." They walked outside with him. "I have a plan."

CHAPTER 17

Twisted

"It will take two more days for me to complete what I have in mind. I didn't want to talk about it in there. Give me an hour, and I will meet you at the Froth after I get a little more done on it." Bick turned and walked back inside.

The girls were walking back hesitantly to J.R.'s store. Sarah said, "They took my phone, along with a lot of other stuff, you know."

"I can't believe they did what they did! Bick's plan better involve a vehicle of some sort! I think we should walk out of here if it doesn't."

"I'm with you! This is just too weird." Sarah then asked, "Do you remember what your mother said? We thought she was talking about aliens?"

"She wasn't talking about immigrants from other countries, you know!" Jessie snapped, "She was talking about UFO aliens from space—outer space!"

"I know!" Sarah shot back. "She was saying something about don't take the short way, go the long way or they will be there. Remember?"

"I said she's nuts! Don't listen to her! I can't believe they're considering letting her out of the ward, man. Now that's freakin weird. She's a mental case!"

Just then they heard the train whistle again. They stopped and looked toward where the sound came from. They spotted Daniel. They turned and continued walking to J.R.'s.

Daniel sang in his girlish voice, "*Girls*—or should I say . . . *ladies."* He walked toward them. "I saw you!" Daniel said sharply.

"So what!" Jessie snapped and turned to walk away.

Daniel demanded, "I think you *girls* really need to stop and *listen* to what I *am* going to tell you."

"Why should we?" Sarah snapped.

"Screw you!" Jessie yelled at the same time.

"Bick is *nuts*, ladies. That is why I *cannot* believe you parked your Volkswagen inside his auto shop." Daniel said. "*He* has trashed a lot of automobiles . . . ask anybody."

Jessie and Sarah stopped in their tracks and turned to face Daniel. "What?" Jessie asked. She noticed red dots staring at them from in between the buildings where Daniel had come from.

Jessie questioned, "Are you saying Bick trashed my bus, Daniel?"

"Yes, precisely. What kind of person washes *his* dead car every week? We believe he did away with his wife and daughter . . . but cannot prove it . . . yet."

"And we should believe you? *Why*?" Jessie insistently asked.

"I am not the crazy *one*, drinking all the time and doing *God* only knows what else."

Jessie said, "No. You just hang out with that little . . ."

Sarah stopped her. "Jessie!"

"What?"

"Stop and listen to what Daniel is saying," Sarah answered.

"Thank *you*, Sarah." Daniel said with a smile. "My word, she *does* get testy."

At that moment, Featus ran from between the buildings. His eyes were glowing bright red. They looked more like an animal's eyes than a human's. He stopped just behind Daniel. Daniel put his hand in front of Featus's face. Featus ran back between the buildings.

Daniel continued, "You see, *ladies*, Bick broke *your* car so he can fix it. And then, he will have *your* trust. And then, well, I just do not know. Like I said, we cannot find a *thing* on his wife and daughter."

"Are you guys even looking for them?" Jessie snarled.

"Maybe . . . just maybe, well, *he* ate them!" Daniel cackled.

Sarah said, "That's crazy, Daniel."

"I know, that is what *I* am saying."

"This whole town is nuts, man," Jessie snapped.

"Like *you* would know about being around nuts, *Jessie*," Daniel said.

"What in the hell does that mean? Daniel!"

"Take it like you will," Daniel said. "Is she always this high-strung, Sarah?"

Sarah replied with a shrug. "We're going back to J.R.'s." They turned to walk away. Sarah turned back, "Is there a phone I can use around here? We need to call our parents. Somebody stole mine out of the bus."

Daniel smiled. "The last thing I heard is that the phone lines are down. Why, you should ask J.R."

"Yeah, right," Sarah said as she turned to walk away.

As they were walking, Jessie asked Sarah, "How can you be so nice to that prick?"

"It doesn't do any good to be the Mega Bitch. You need to chill out! Don't talk if you're going to be a smart ass. Why don't you listen to me, for a change?"

"I'll try. Hey, man, do you think he could have heard our conversation about my mom being nuts?"

"No way! It was coincidental he said what he said. You really need to chill out." Sarah looked back and saw Daniel and Featus staring after them.

CHAPTER 18

Bitten

When they walked inside the store, J.R. jumped from behind the counter with a guilty look on his face. "Bah-ha."

"Yeah, Bah to you too," Jessie said.

Sarah slapped Jessie's arm.

"Well, what's the scoop-bah on all the . . . poop-bah-ha-ha?"

"Jessie and I are confused," Sarah said.

"Triple L . . . remember! Go with your first feelings. Don't let the facts freak you . . ." J.R. was mumbling.

"I can't stand this for much longer," Jessie was saying. "I can't understand you guys. Shit! We need a phone, man. I can't believe this shit hole of a town doesn't even have a phone that works."

"Well, foooorrr . . ." J.R. was saying, then began to stare out the window as a black Suburban was heading for the other end of town.

Sarah and Jessie quickly turned around and spotted the SUV. Sarah asked J.R. instantly, "Is that the ranger?"

"Yes-bah . . . what a . . . mess-bah-ha."

The train whistle sounded.

"Do you hear that, J.R.?" Sarah asked.

"Bah, bah, bah, bah . . ."

The girls turned to look where J.R. was staring. At the door stood Daniel. Featus was running around in circles right outside the door.

Sarah asked, "Is that the ranger that just drove by, Daniel?"

"Where in the hell is the train, Daniel?" Jessie asked sharply.

"What? No hello? I guess we were not taught any manners . . . my, my. This just will not do," Daniel said, shaking his head.

"Maybe we should just go down and speak with the Ranger, Jessie," Sarah said.

"Suit yourselves, ladies," Daniel barked.

"We will!" Sarah snarled.

That instant, Featus pulled open the door and screeched, "I want to feed!"

"You heard Featus, give him what he wants, J.R.!" Daniel said.

J.R. answered, "But-bah. It's so small-bah, nothing at . . . all-bah."

Daniel demanded, "Give Featus what he wants!"

Sarah started to protest, "He'll just ki—"

J.R. cut her off, "It's the last . . . bah. It's, you know-bah. Extinct-bah. The last from the past-bah."

"I know you don't expect me to get all sentimental and teary-eyed," Daniel smirked. "Now! Give Featus what he wants!"

"Don't do it, J.R., that little freak will just k—" Jessie was saying.

J.R. snapped, "It's mine-bah. Don't whine-bah. It will be an honor-bah, to give it to Featus-bah. I'm sure he will enjoy-bah his new toy-bah-ha-ha."

The black SUV drove back by the other way. Jessie questioned, "Is that Bick with the ranger?"

Daniel just glared at Jessie, tapping his fingers against his chin.

J.R. walked back with the kitten in his hand. He had tears in his eyes.

Featus's eyes were glowing bloodred as he ran to J.R. beaming with excitement.

Sarah inquired, "Are you going to give him the bottle too, J.R?"

"I do not really think Featus-bah needs a bottle-bah-ha." J.R. said. "He is not a baby, after all, bah-ha-ha."

J.R. bent down to give Featus the kitten. Featus grabbed the kitten and bit J.R.'s arm. He broke the skin with his teeth. It started to bleed.

"Bah!"

Featus ran past everybody and out the door. He turned right and headed toward the cemetery. Daniel spun on his heels and strolled out the door, as if nothing had happened.

Jessie shouted, "Where is the ranger taking Bick?"

Daniel waved back at her, not even turning to look at her.

She turned to J.R., "Where? Do you know where? Why did you give *it* the kitten?"

J.R. was holding his arm, trying to stop the bleeding. "You girls don't get it-bah. They . . . run it-bah. Everything-bah. Every dog has its . . . day-bah. He'll . . . pay-bah. Bah-ha-ha, bah-ha-ha. He bit me-bah. Bah-ha-ha."

Sarah got something off the shelf to doctor his arm. As she was bandaging the wound, she asked, "Are you ready to get out of here?"

"I want to . . . retreat-bah, but can't do it-bah, with only my feet-bah. We won't escape-bah this rape without Bick-bah-ha."

The girls were supposed to meet Bick in less than a half hour. They weren't sure where the ranger took him or why or even for how long.

"Who else can we trust, J.R.?" Sarah questioned.

"Everybody is so scared-bah, that they won't be . . . spared-bah. Think that Daniel and the ranger know it . . . all-bah. It makes my skin crawl-bah. They might be right-bah. Ow . . . my bite-bah-ha-ha. They knew you two would be . . . comin-bah, before you even . . . thought you'd have to be runnin bah-ha."

"How did they know?" Jessie asked.

J.R. shrugged it off.

"How did they know?" Jessie demanded.

"Daniel . . . told me to expect the . . . unexpected-bah. You girls are . . . unprotected-bah."

"We need to get out of here! Are you with us or what?" Jessie asked harshly.

"Bah . . . yes . . . I guess-bah."

"We'll go down to the Froth to see if Bick shows up. I'll check my bus to see if I can get it going. If it runs, we'll take it. If it doesn't run, I am walking out of here. What do you say, man?"

"Not too wise . . . bah, guys-bah."

"Why is that, J.R?" Jessie challenged.

"Bick's family had . . . a car-bah, they didn't get very . . . far-bah-ha."

"What should we do then, J.R? I can't stand this for another night. It seems like years already." Sarah cried.

"No . . . dear-bah. I . . . fear-bah, it's a . . . mere twenty-four hours, bah-ha-ha."

"J.Rrrr . . ." Jessie started to say.

"Just wait for . . . Bick-bah, then we'll . . . skate . . . quick-bah-ha-ha, bah-ha-ha."

CHAPTER 19

The Undertaker

"How do we know that we're not being jerked around by everybody in this . . . place?" Sarah asked Jessie as they walked back to the Froth Finder.

"We don't know. I do know one thing, though, the church is way too far to walk to. We would never make it. J.R. was right about that. Let's go to the shop to check out the bus before we go to the Froth," Jessie said.

They entered the shop. Jessie went to the engine compartment and noticed the belt was cut. She checked in the side box for the spare, it too was cut. "Shit, man! They cut the spare too! I can't take much more of this crap. Let's ask everybody if anybody has a phone. And then we'll just wait for Bick. We will get out, Sarah! Somehow, we will get out!"

Thunder crashed! It shook the building. They ran to the Froth. It had started to sprinkle. They opened the door, everybody turned to look at them. Jessie asked loudly, "Does anybody here have a phone or know anybody that might have one that is actually working?" The townspeople turned back around and continued doing what they had been doing before Sarah and Jessie walked in.

Jessie asked the bartender, "Is your phone still down?"

"Sorry to say, it is."

As they were heading toward the restroom, an elderly woman got up and walked in front of them to go to the restroom. The lady handed them a note.

Jessie and Sarah read, *"There are no phones in this town that work anymore."*

Jessie started to say something; the lady grabbed the note back and wrote.

Jessie and Sarah read, *"If you get out, send back help. Nobody ever leaves here!"*

Jessie nodded yes. The lady took the note, went to the toilet and burned it. She finished her business in there and left. Sarah nosed toward the door, and they exited.

Jessie walked out first. She noticed the black SUV driving past the Froth, heading away from Bick's shop. Jessie took off running out the door, Sarah trailing behind her. It was too late. The vehicle was already at the graveyard. Jessie and Sarah looked at Bick standing there with a smashed-up motorcycle and a body lying on the ground. They turned and looked back at the bar, everybody was still sitting. Save two men.

The two men came strolling out of the Froth Finder. They walked over to Bick. On the other side of the street, a light came on in a building that looked empty. The sign on the door read **UNDERTAKER**. A man walked out. He was dressed in a black suit with a top hat. He directed the two men to take the body into his shop.

Bick started to drag the motorcycle. The girls ran over to him and helped him drag it inside the shop.

"Bick, what happened?" Sarah asked.

"I guess he crashed," he said, then he mumbled, "I'm gunna drain the gas and get the battery and whatever else is good yet." He went back to his regular voice, "Will you two help me push your van to the junkyard? It's behind the shop here."

"What?" Jessie shrieked, "You can fix it!"

"No. We have no belts or batteries for it. That tire is mostly flat." Then he whispered, "I have a plan."

Bick opened the garage door where the Volkswagen was parked. He released the emergency brake and began to push it. Three men and a woman came out of the bar to help them. The elderly woman got inside to steer it. They drove it behind the shop to the junkyard.

Sarah noticed that the vehicles were in fairly good shape; in fact a lot of them were not even wrecked. The ones that were wrecked could have been fixed easily anywhere else. She asked as they were walking back around the building, "What is this? A graveyard for healthy-looking cars?"

They all looked at her and smiled; two of the guys just nodded.

Bick said, "There's not much you can do with a trashed engine and nothing as far as a part to fix it."

"Well?" Jessie asked Bick as they approached the shop door.

"Let me take care of this bike before we meet at the Froth." And then he whispered, "I don't want to leave it for long, something will happen to it." In his normal voice he said, "You girls go to the Froth." He whispered, "Wait for me there."

The girls went back to the Froth and asked for a root beer float. The bartender laughed and gave them a cup of coffee. "Drink up, ladies. I fear a storm is on the way." Just then it thundered.

A few people got up and left. Sarah and Jessie went to the back, sat down, and waited for Bick.

The thunder grew louder.

CHAPTER 20

Boothill of Automobiles

The storm was getting closer. The bartender and the girls were left. The bartender put his raincoat on and said, "Well, I'm closing now. You girls need to get to where you're going. This is going to be a bad one." They got up and walked out. He shouted, "See ya tonight!"

"Not if we can help it!" Jessie hollered back.

The bartender laughed and jogged off across the street.

Bick met them at the door. He stepped out. The thunder sounded. "I am building a vehicle out of the old automobiles in the junk yard. The best part, well . . . not for you two, is that you had gas in your van. I drained it out before they had time to ruin it."

"Where is it?" Jessie asked.

"I siphoned it into gas cans."

"No, I mean where is the car you're building?"

"Oh yeah, in my house. Well in the bedroom, to be exact."

"How will you get it out?" Sarah asked.

"When we get ready to go, we drive it right through the walls! We don't stop until we get help. I've been working on this for quite some time, you see. Without sleep, two more days at the most, tomorrow most likely. I have to sleep for a couple of hours. And then I'll try to finish it. OK?"

"We have no choice!" Jessie retorted.

"Yes, OK." Sarah said. "He's doing what he can, Jessie."

"Yeah," Jessie said.

"You girls go to J.R. and tell him it will be within a couple of days." Bick warned. "Don't say anything else to anyone, no matter what!"

"We won't," Sarah answered. They took off running to J.R.'s as Bick locked the door.

The rumbling grew louder.

CHAPTER 21

Segundo Dia

J.R. locked the door after them. They walked to the back. He picked up the box, which held the two kittens, and handed it to Sarah. They went inside his house. J.R. locked both doors. When they were in the hallway, he said, "Got some . . . good news-bah to clear these . . . blues-bah? Bah-ha."

"A couple of days," Jessie responded.

"Good day," J.R. mumbled. He turned leaving them standing in the hallway and walked into his bedroom, shut his door, and locked it.

Jessie and Sarah lit the candles in their room and fed the kittens. Jessie picked up the one she had sleeping on her chest the day before and petted it.

"I can't believe this is only the second night here. It feels we've been here so long, I can't take much more of this, Sarah. We've got to get out of here, man. I don't want to sleep either because of that dream, man, it was so real." Jessie shivered.

"It was only a dream." Sarah tried to comfort Jessie.

"It didn't feel like it, Sarah."

Sarah put the kittens in the box and put it in the drawer. She lay down and slept.

Jessie sat there with her knees drawn up against her chest, her arms around her legs, rocking back and forth. She was thinking what her mother had said about going off the path and taking the shortcut. *How could she have known? There is just no way!* She was trying to convince herself in her own mind. *She's just a crazy woman*, she kept repeating over and over in her mind. Rocking back and forth, back and forth . . . "Oh, Mom, I should've listened, should've listened . . ." she found herself saying out loud. "We need help, man, we need help . . ." repeating over and over.

Sarah was tossing and turning, sweating profusely. The kittens began to meow. Jessie heard them and stopped rocking. She noticed Sarah tossing and turning; she put her hand on Sarah's forehead and told her it was only a dream and that everything is all right. Sarah calmed a little.

Jessie got up to feed the kittens. She told the kittens that they would be safe! She would see to that! With Bick's help, they will leave! She began to talk out loud again. "Maybe one day, maybe two, we will be gone and this place will be the past!" *The first thing is to call my sister and then my mother,* she thought. I will let them know everything is just fine and that I love them. Both! "The opposite of love is not hate but indifference. I don't hate my mother after all! I love her and want her well!" She made a mental note of this. She finished feeding the kittens.

Jessie walked back to the bed where Sarah was sweating, tossing, and turning. She was incoherent and rambling on. Jessie tried to shake her awake. Sarah began swinging at Jessie. "Get them off! They're killing me!" Jessie held her arms down and reassured her everything was fine. Sarah slowly became rational.

"What time is it, Jessie?"

"I don't know. What was your dream?"

"I never want to sleep again. I know what you were talking about now. It was the same as your dream last night." She got ready to go. "Did you dream?"

"No, I really didn't sleep," Jessie told her as she handed Sarah the box holding the kittens.

CHAPTER 22

You Again

The doors leading to the store were unlocked. J.R. was pulling up the blinds. Jessie said, "Hi, J.R."

"Bah! You shocked me! Bah . . . you should have . . . knocked-bah!"

"You need to hide these," Jessie said as she took the box from Sarah.

"Yes . . . bah. I have the purr-fect place-bah, for the furry . . . face-bah-ha."

Jessie rolled her eyes and shook her head.

Sarah stepped in front of Jessie and asked, "Do you sleep at all, J.R.?"

"Well . . . hell-bah, not very . . . well-bah. After a . . . while-bah, it's no B.F.D. just another day . . . on the dial-bah. You learn to live with it . . . bah, just take it . . . when they give it-bah."

"No, we won't, J.R.," Jessie shot back. "We're going to find Bick and help him so we can get gone! Today!"

J.R. put the kittens in a different box with a lid. He placed it behind the counter. "It's padded-bah. They won't hear them . . . cry-bah. I just . . . added-bah, don't ask me . . . to lie-bah-ha-ha, bah-ha."

"You're going with, aren't you, J.R.?" Sarah questioned.

"Ab ab ab ab ab," J.R. repeated over and over.

The girls turned quickly, and there stood Daniel. "Are you going somewhere, J.R.? Ladies?"

"Oh . . . no-bah. Where do I . . . dare go-bah? You know-bah."

69

"Why are you always slinking up on people, Daniel?" questioned Jessie.

"Oh, honey . . ."

"I'm not your honey!" shouted Jessie.

"Oh forgive me, Ms. Jessie. I thought I would come to give you the news. Of course, I do not want you to hear it from just, anyone." Daniel sassed.

"Give me the . . . clues-bah, about the . . . sad news-bah-ha-ha."

"Well," Daniel said, drumming his fingers against his lips, "Well now . . . let me see . . . how do I begin . . . ?"

"What is it, Featus ran away?" Jessie laughed sarcastically.

"No . . . let me see now . . ." Daniel, slowly come to the point, said, "It is about Bick."

At that moment, Featus came running in from the direction of the graveyard. He swung the door open and ran past Daniel. He stood in front of the girls, smiling and sniffing up in the air.

"What's he doing?" Sarah asked, while taking a step back away from Featus.

Jessie also took a step back.

Featus just stood there, sniffing the air over his head.

Daniel said, "Today was Featus's first day of school. He is being prepared for his new bride."

"Bride?" Jessie shrieked.

"Oh yes. Very soon, little Master Featus will wed. His future bride is not yet born. You see, in *their* culture, they arrange the marriages from the day their bride is conceived. We *were* awaiting the arrival of the surrogate mothers." Daniel explained. "Do you get it? J.R., give Featus what he wants," he said, sounding bored.

"What happened to Bick?" Sarah asked, while keeping her eyes on Featus, who was still sniffing the air.

"You guys are a bunch of freaks!" Jessie wailed.

J.R. cut in, "Bah-bah-bah . . ."

Daniel said again, "Give Featus what he wants, J.R."

Just then the black SUV drove by, towing a vehicle.

Jessie grabbed Sarah's arm and led her around Featus. "Let's go. I think it's time to talk to the ranger."

"Suit yourselves," Daniel said in a snooty voice. "He is in a very *foul* mood after what happened to Bick."

Featus went and stood in front of J.R., still sniffing over his head.

"Screw you, Daniel!" Jessie said as they rushed by him.

"No, but the ranger will!" Daniel hollered as they exited. "Give Featus what he wants!"

J.R. reached into the box for one of the kittens. He started to pick up the one that Jessie had held the first night. The kitten bit and scratched J.R., and he dropped it. He picked up the other one. J.R. was shaking, with tears in his eyes, when he handed the kitten to Featus. He asked Daniel, "What's the . . . deal-bah with Bick, did something . . . real-kick? Bah."

Featus took the kitten and was holding it close to his chest. His eyes were glowing bloodred again, with that grin on his face.

Daniel turned to walk out, ignoring J.R. Featus followed right behind him, squeezing the kitten to his chest now. They turned right, toward the graveyard. After Daniel disappeared, J.R. went outside. He watched as the girls approach the SUV.

The ranger was unhooking that weird-looking vehicle from his truck. He was bending down, finishing up.

"Excuse me, ranger?" Sarah said. The ranger stood up and turned around to face Sarah and Jessie. He was grinning. "Preacher? You're the ranger?"

"So here we meet again. How have you been treated in our quaint little town?" the ranger/preacher asked, sarcastically.

"We're trying to . . ." Sarah began to say.

The ranger interrupted, "Did I not warn you? Why, you wouldn't listen because you know it all! Your generation knows everything! Why listen to anyone! I warned you, and it was your choice to come here. Wasn't it?" He would not wait for an answer. "Now you can deal with it! We're just the small fish, the monkey's out of the bag, if you will." He was laughing. "We are watching a new beginning. No! We are taking *part* in the new beginning! You both will be a huge part of it. I'm hoping only one of you will because I want Sarah as my own! But unfortunately it will most likely be both of you. Oh yes,

I'm sure. It took four last time." He laughed again. "What a shame, two beautiful women such as you are."

Jessie shoved past Sarah and said, "Slow down, man. Just what are you saying?"

The ranger reached out and grabbed Jessie by the hair. Sarah stepped up and tried to free Jessie, yelling for him to let go. The ranger put Jessie in a headlock and held both her hands with his right hand. He shoved Sarah against the SUV and held her there with his left hand against her neck.

"You!" he said to Sarah, while Jessie was yelling and fighting to free herself. "You I want, but will never get to experience. After you do what you came here to do, you will go down in history! If that's any consolation. You will have made a name for yourselves. 'The mothers of the new beginning.' Has a nice ring to it, don't you think? Oh my, I see why Featus likes this one." He shoved Jessie back about ten feet, and she fell so hard it knocked the wind out of her. That freed the ranger's right arm. He grabbed Sarah with both hands and licked her face.

The train whistle sounded.

He shoved Sarah into Jessie, who was now standing. He got into his vehicle and drove off. As the ranger drove by J.R.'s store, J.R. turned around quickly and pretended to be washing the windows. After the ranger was out of sight, J.R. ran over to the girls.

"Are you OK . . . bah to play . . . Sarah-bah? Jessie, it could get . . . messy-bah."

"What was that?" Jessie commanded.

"That's the . . . ranger-bah, we're in . . . danger-bah."

They heard a moan from the back of the vehicle the ranger had just left. They ran to the back. It was Bick, tied to the trunk.

"Bick," Jessie said loudly. "What happened? Why didn't you wait for us, Bick?"

Bick was struggling to say something. Sarah got close so she could hear what Bick was whispering, while Jessie was untying his hands. "I left a note for you girls at the shop, explaining everything. I'm sorry. I had to try to save my family."

"Is there a doctor, J.R? Get the doctor," Sarah said and then told Bick, "Try not to talk."

"Too late for me, Sarah. Wife's gone, daughter . . ." he choked.

Sarah helped him to his side. He was coughing. She began patting his back. "Slow, Bick, you're going to be all right."

"No," Bick continued. "Daughter's a guinea pig. It's not her, my daughter. Being used." He coughed again. "Incubator, that's all, she . . ."

"J.R., is there a doctor?!" Sarah demanded.

"No, doctor-bah. Only . . . stocker-bah."

People were gathering around now. J.R. walked back to his store.

Bick urged, "Listen to me!" Sarah and Jessie got closer to Bick. "There is no time left. There is no train! Don't follow the whistle . . ." Bick died.

CHAPTER 23

Sarah

Sarah started shaking Bick, "Don't die, Bick. We need you. We need you, Bick . . ."

Jessie led Sarah away from Bick. The guy from the undertaker's office came out with a body bag and instructed two men to help him take care of it. Four other people pushed the strange-looking vehicle back behind the shop.

Sarah and Jessie stepped back, away from the crowd. "We've got to get out of here, Sarah."

"That was our chance, right there, Jessie. Why didn't he wait? Maybe with all of us, we would have a chance. We could have made it. We don't even have a car or anything now. We're stuck, Jessie, stuck." Sarah's head was hanging down. She wiped the tears from her eyes.

Jessie stepped closer to Sarah and grabbed her arms, "Don't do this, Sarah. We will get out! We just have to change the plan—"

Sarah interrupted, "You don't re—"

Jessie roared, "No! Don't say it! We will get out! Let's go talk to J.R." She grabbed Sarah's hand and dragged her to J.R.'s store.

J.R. was waiting at the door. "Tell me-bah, what will . . . it be-bah?"

Jessie said, "J.R., Bick is dead."

"I seen . . . bah, the phean-bah. Bick bit the . . . dust-bah, just like that . . . quick-bah-ha-ha."

"We're still leaving, J.R. Are you going with us?" Jessie asked.

"There's no . . . hope-bah, might as well get . . . the rope-bah. Or get me the . . . dope-bah-ha-ha."

Sarah questioned J.R., "Isn't there another way?"

J.R. said, "I don't, d, d, d . . ."

Jessie and Sarah turned to face Daniel standing at the door. Featus was walking back and forth just outside the door, behind Daniel.

Daniel taunted, "Well, well, ladies. I see you finally met the ranger."

Sarah said harshly, "He's the preacher!"

"What are you talking about, little miss?" Daniel questioned.

"You know what she's saying, Daniel, you fake . . ." Jessie was saying.

"Now, now Jessica, did you forget your pills? Again?"

"Screw you, Daniel!" Jessie shot back.

At that moment, Featus ripped the door open, ran past Daniel and the girls to J.R., and screeched, "I want to feed!" He was holding his hand out toward the box that held the last kitten.

J.R. reached in and picked up the remaining kitten. He started to hand it to Featus. As Featus reached for it, Sarah screamed, "No! Featus, leave it!" She put her hands over her face and sobbed.

Featus walked over to her. In a soft voice, he said, "Sarah." He put his head down and stood in front of her with a sad look on his face. She took the horseshoe from her back pocket and handed it to Featus. Featus took it, then looked back down at the floor.

Daniel yelled at Sarah, "Do not dare speak to Featus in that fashion!"

Featus looked up at Sarah with bewilderment on his face.

Sarah stumbled over her words, "It's j-just a-a b-baby."

Daniel hooted, "Oh, I hear J.R.'s speech impediment is contagious!"

Featus turned slowly toward Daniel, his eyes gleaming bright red. Featus hissed. All eyes were upon him as he walked at a slug's pace toward Daniel.

Daniel, with the arrogant look on his face, held out a cross in front of Featus's face. Featus put his hands in front of his face, looking as if to block the sight of the cross. He turned his face sideways. Featus then began sneering and laughing lightly. He held the horseshoe up toward Daniel's face and laughed harder. His eyes were still glittering with red. Now he was baring his teeth. He put the horseshoe to his side and took Daniel's hand in his and led him out the door. Before they exited, Featus turned back to Sarah and said in an undertone, "Sarah." They turned right and went the same way they normally went, toward the graveyard.

Doomed

"What the-bah."

"Yeah!" Jessie answered, "Bah."

"That's weird!" Sarah said.

"Now what?" Jessie asked.

J.R. answered in a mumble, "Never before-bah. Never again-ba-haha." He put the kitten back in the box.

Jessie added, "Doesn't that abnormal grow an inch or two every time we see him?"

"Yeah, that's what I'm saying!" Sarah answered.

"We've got to get out! Like, now!" Jessie persisted. "Let's go find the note Bick left at the shop."

Sarah asked, "Are you going, J.R., with or without a car?"

"You get the . . . note-bah, see what Bick . . . wrote-bah. Bring it . . . back-bah, and we'll . . . react-bah-ha-ha."

"Get ready. Be ready," Jessie told J.R. as they went out the door.

The street was cleared of all the evidence that Bick had died and of his makeshift car. They walked quickly to the shop. They began to look for the note. "Do you think it's inside the house part?" Sarah asked.

There was a big hole in the wall where Bick had driven the car through the wall. "No, man, he said the shop." Jessie pulled the roll-up blind down on the door's window. The note fell to the ground. "I've got it, Sarah." They read it as they walked to the Froth Finder.

The note read:

I went to get my family. Daniel is on our side, after all. He saw them, and he told me where to look. It's by the train tracks at the crossing. He's going to meet me there to save them. I will send help back when we get out. I couldn't wait. You will be free soon.

Bick

They finished reading the note as they got to the Froth door. They stopped at the door. "Bullshit!" Jessie yelled.

A lady they had never seen before walked out. She kept her head down as she walked between them and said, quickly and quietly, "Why don't you believe me? Your mother knows." She turned right and headed down toward J.R.'s end of town.

Sarah and Jessie looked at her strangely, shook their heads and opened the door. As they walked in, Sarah said, "That freak Daniel set Bick up."

"He still could have waited!" Jessie hollered. "Or come and got us from J.R.'s!"

"If it's not one thing, it will be another! Now we have nothing! No car to leave in, no way to go!" Sarah was expressing herself, loudly. They were walking to the restroom.

The bartender asked, "Hey girls, you OK?"

"BS!" Sarah shrieked at him. They entered the restroom. Sarah leaned against the sink, while Jessie went into a stall. "What was he thinking? Who knows if we would have ever gotten the note if that prick didn't kill him here? That bartender is probably on their side, anyway! Everybody is! We're doomed! Did you hear me, Jessie? Doomed, with a capital D-O-O-M-E-D!"

Jessie walked over to the sink. As she was washing her hands, she said, "We just need to rethink everything, man. After what Featus . . ." Jessie stopped in mid-sentence, when the door opened.

The lady that had come in the first night entered. She handed Jessie a note. Then went into a stall.

Jessie read: *DON'T TALK IN HERE!*

"What's going on with this shit hole of a town?" Jessie demanded.

The lady walked out, took the note from Jessie, went to the toilet, and burned the note. She flushed it and then answered, "Nothing is different than always. It's always this exciting. Or boring, depending on how you look at it." Then she exited.

The girls followed her out the door. The woman went and sat with two men. Jessie and Sarah walked out and over to the restaurant. They ordered and took the food to J.R.'s. They gave him his meal and stood around the counter, eating.

Featus shoved the door open and screeched at the top of his lungs, "I want to feed!"

Daniel walked in. He was a jumbled mess. He had no crosses on. His pants were ripped and dirty. His tuxedo shirt was in shreds. And his face was cut and bruised. One of his ears was torn a quarter of the way off and bleeding. The other ear had the earring ripped out and was also bleeding. One of his eyes was swollen shut. His lips were so fat, he couldn't open his mouth. He had cuts all over his body, especially where his clothes were ripped. Whatever had cut the clothes also cut his skin.

Sarah, Jessie, and J.R. just stood there in horror. J.R. just kept repeating, "Bah-bah . . ."

CHAPTER 25

Bleeding Crosses

Sarah looked from Daniel to Featus, then back again. Featus smiled at Sarah and whispered, "Sarah." Sarah handed one of the watches to Featus. He took it and smiled. The train whistle blew.

Featus turned and ran out past Daniel. As he ran by, he slugged him in the stomach. Daniel doubled over. As he was straightening back up, the girls and J.R. noticed something shiny coming out from between his lips.

"What is . . ." Jessie began. She moved closer to Daniel.

That's when she noticed a lump crawling under his skin on his neck. It was moving toward his jaw. Another shiny object was coming out of his skin in his jaw. Daniel's eyes widened with fear and pain. The lump forced the object out. It fell to the floor. It was one of the crosses, which he once wore. The one fell from his lips. The lump started moving toward his arm, heading for another shiny cross working its way out of his skin.

"Daniel!" Jessie exclaimed.

Daniel's face distorted, eyes wide in terror, screaming in excruciating agony.

Featus came running back into the store. He jumped in front of Jessie and hissed, baring his teeth.

Jessie jumped back, next to Sarah.

Featus ran into Daniel. He hit him in the leg hard with his shoulder. Daniel fell to the floor. Featus grabbed his shirt collar and dragged him out like he weighed nothing. As he exited, the ranger pulled up and threw Daniel in the backseat of his SUV. Featus got in the front seat. The ranger got in and did a brody to turn around. They took off, away from town.

Jessie took a closer look at the floor and said, "He's bleeding crosses!" She turned to J.R. and Sarah. J.R. was removing all his crosses and putting them in a drawer.

The thunder began to roll again. Sheets of rain were falling. Lightning struck everywhere.

J.R. ran and started pulling the shades down. He locked the door. Sarah grabbed the box that held the kitten. Then went and opened the back door which led to the house. Jessie was following. As the door was closing behind them, Jessie heard J.R. yell something. She turned quickly to ask what he was saying. As she turned, she noticed the front door closing behind him.

"J.R!" Jessie screamed. She reached the front door and slammed outside. "J.R!"

CHAPTER 26

Forgiveness

J.R. was getting inside an old car. It was raining so hard and the car was already in front of the post office. Jessie couldn't make out what kind of car it was or who was in the driver's seat. She was running to try to catch up but couldn't. Sarah was running after her. The car flipped around and took off at a high speed toward the graveyard. The water on the ground splashed up on Jessie and Sarah as the car sped by. Lightning was striking all around.

The girls rushed back to the store. Sarah went back to the kitten. Jessie locked the front door. They went to the house. Jessie started to deadbolt it. Sarah said, "Maybe we shouldn't deadbolt it, what if J.R. comes back?"

Jessie took the deadbolt off. "But what if whatever he locks out comes in?" She put the deadbolt back on.

"I don't know, Jessie."

"He won't come back." Jessie persuaded Sarah. She finished locking all the locking devices.

"Where do you think he went?"

"Away from here, man. Away from here." Jessie answered, sounding totally burned out. As they were walking back to their room, Jessie said, "What is it with that freak? I think he did that to Daniel because of what he said to you." "He did."

"You know that, for sure?" Asked Jessie.

"Yeah, I do."

"How?"

"It's kind of weird, but it's like . . . Featus can talk directly to my brain. He's in love with me and won't let anybody hurt me. I think he's transforming into . . . something. And I don't know what." Sarah said.

The candles were lit. Jessie picked up the kitten to pet it. "Like what? Is that why you give him something when he stands in front of you?" She put the kitten down and fed it.

"Yes, but he wants more, Jessie. I can feel it, and he can read what I'm thinking too. I think, anyway."

"What do you think?"

"I try not to think of anything but the beach. I don't want him to know how I actually feel or what I really think. We've got to figure out a way to leave! I have a horrific feeling, Jessie." Sarah was not going to tell Jessie exactly what she was thinking. She knew they had to leave. And soon.

Jessie picked up the kitten as Sarah lay down. "I am going to lie here and rest my eyes. If I doze, wake me quickly. OK, Jessie? I don't want to dream."

"Yeah, I will. No way am I going to sleep or even rest my eyes, man." Jessie leaned back with the kitten on her chest.

She was stroking the kitten and thinking about the past. While she was growing up, there had been some bizarre times. Realizing what a unique upbringing she had. *Wild. What a crazy life, with such a crazy mother. Plenty of good times, though. There were more good times than bad.* But, when her mother was diagnosed with schizophrenia and put in the hospital, "Oh, man!" *It really wasn't happening, it couldn't be for real.* The bona fide problem was, *her mother was an old hippie and had done way too many drugs in the day. That's what it had been!* Jessie was sure of it. They put her mother in the hospital, pumped her full of drugs. *Thank you very much doctors* and said she was a nut. Now that she is a legal drug addict, they've got her where they want her. *When we get out of this mess we're in, if we get out alive . . .* "Bellowing Hollers! Shit!" *I will get my mother out of the prison that they put her in! So what if she likes to have a little more fun than most mothers. Really, she enjoys more fun than most people.* She laughed out loud. "Why is that a crime?" She felt better now that she made amends with her mother, at least in her heart. She felt better. She lay back with the kitten sleeping on her. The thunder growing louder, she was lost in thought.

She slept.

CHAPTER 27

Daydreaming

As they lay there, sleeping, they both began to dream.

Sarah was dreaming, not only of the one dream everybody dreamed in their sleep, but also of a faint meow. *It is a kitten*, she thought, but could not wake. Her slumber deepened. *A massage. Oh, yes*. It felt as though she was receiving a massage, a full body rub-down. Falling, falling, fall . . .

As Jessie slept, she also heard the faint meow of a kitten. Like Sarah, she was being massaged. The meow was fading, fading . . . she began to spin. As she was falling, when she suddenly felt a bite on her chin. She screamed and heard Sarah's earsplitting scream as well, but could not respond or even move.

A bite on her chin again. She sat straight up, opened her eyes to darkness, and reached over to Sarah, shaking her aggressively, yelling, "Sarah, wake! Sarah!" There were black fuzzy things all over Sarah. "Oh man, Sarah! You've got to wake up!" She then realized not only were they on Sarah, but they were on her too! They were all over the bed. The kitten meowed. Sarah was blaring out earth-shattering screams. Jessie reached in her pocket for a match. She was shaking fiercely. Strike one—it wouldn't light. Trembling. "If I can't light this, we will die." The kitten meow was shrieking. The train whistle sounded. Strike two—"It won't light! Sarah, wake up, please!" Meow. Strike three—the sizzle of the match lighting.

Sarah sat straight up, letting out a final bellow. The kitten was still hissing and meowing angrily.

"Give me the candle, Sarah!"

Sarah reached blindly in what little light the match let out. She found it and handed it to Jessie. She got another candle, lit it, and placed it on the dresser. And then another.

Jessie was searching for the kitten. There were fuzzy balls all over the bed; she was tossing them off, searching radically for the kitten. In her haste she glanced quickly to the corner of the room where there was no light. She saw the red glowing eyes, the same as the ones they had seen the night they had been camping. The night that Steve had died . . . she looked away hastily. She rubbed her chin and felt blood!

"What bit you?"

"I don't know."

"Meow."

"It was the kitten, Sarah!"

"Meow," the kitten was pouncing toward Jessie from the end of the bed. Jessie reached for it. "Meow." There was a little blood around the kitten's mouth. Jessie held it close to her heart.

Sarah was searching for more of the fuzzy things and slapping them off the bed. She began lighting all of the candles.

"Shit, Sarah, we almost died in our sleep, and this kitten saved us."

"That was the worse dream yet. Well, actually it wasn't a dream."

"No doubt, man. We've got to go, Sarah."

"I wonder what time it is?" Sarah asked.

CHAPTER 28

Overslept

Jessie got up and ready to go. Sarah was ready and waiting. Jessie put the kitten in her jacket pocket and its food in the other pocket. They walked down the hallway, opened the store door. Looking into the store, it was still dark. No J.R.

"He's gone," Jessie stated the obvious.

"Let's go to the Froth and see if anybody saw anything, like who J.R. left with," Sarah said. They exited the store.

Walking to the other end of town, Sarah said, "I wonder if they ever pick up the mail in this . . . this town?"

"I bet not, let's go across the street and check it out."

"After we go to the Froth and get something to eat," Sarah said. "I am starved. Man, I'm so sick of this hellhole! Should we walk out or what?"

"I'm thinking we should take off right after we eat and find out something about J.R., or anything at all."

"I'm starved, let's eat first. And then we'll jam," Sarah agreed.

They approached the Grease Trap. "Closed!" Jessie exclaimed. "No way, man. It can't be two already. We slept that late?"

"I feel like I had no sleep at all, and I am starved. Weird, man!"

"What is?"

"This. Déjà vu. Oh, never mind. It passed."

"OK, then, let's go to the Froth and see what time it is. And find out whatever we can find out. I'll go see if there is gas left at Bick's, and I'll swipe a belt from one of the other cars back there that may work, at least to leave here. Hopefully find the gas. Without that, we're walking. I'm leaving tonight, anyway I can."

"You think you know how to fix the bus?"

"Somewhat. We'll just figure it out as we go." Jessie sounded very confident. "There are other ways to get around the cut belts. Hell, we'll go to J.R.'s and use pantyhose as a belt."

"Pay up!" Laughed the bartender, to a man they had never seen before.

The man turned, looked at Jessie and Sarah, turned back around, took his wallet out, and handed the bartender some money.

"Thank you," said the bartender, as he put the money in his front pocket.

"Thanks to you girls, I just lost fifty dollars," the man said to the girls.

"What in the hell are you talking about?" Jessie demanded.

The bartender asked, "What happened to your chin?"

"Screw you, what about the fifty dollars and us?" Jessie insisted.

"We bet, I said you girls were still with us, and he said you were gone."

"How would we leave, asshole?" Jessie snarled at the man.

"I didn't say you left, I said you were gone." The man laughed as he turned around and walked toward the door.

"Go to hell!" Jessie roared.

"Ladies seem to go first around here . . . Jessie!" the man quipped as the door closed behind him.

Sarah inquired, "Who was that?"

"He lives here," the bartender responded.

"Do you know who J.R. left with?" Sarah questioned.

"Nope. But if the ranger doesn't know yet that he's gone, shit's really going to hit the fan. I hope I'm not around," said the bartender.

A lady got up from her seat and headed to the restroom. Sarah turned and followed. Jessie started to say something to the bartender, but Sarah grabbed her arm and dragged her to the restroom. It was the same lady as last time. She handed Jessie a note.

Jessie read: *Something is really happening here. That guy that was here is a newcomer. He may be the new Overseer. We don't know for sure.*

Sarah read: *Don't trust the BT! That man knows everybody and seems to know everything.*

The lady snatched the note out of Sarah's hand, took it to the toilet, burned it, and flushed it. She was walking out when Jessie asked, "How do you know who to trust?"

"Go with your first feelings," she said before the door closed completely.

"But listen . . ." Sarah had started to say. It was too late.

"Shit!" Jessie yelped.

Sarah answered with, "No shit."

They used the restroom, washed their hands, and walked out.

CHAPTER 29

Taken

Everybody was outside when they walked out. "What in the . . ." Jessie was saying as she took her jacket off and handed it to Sarah. "Hold this!" she said as she headed for the door, running.

"What?" Sarah cried and followed after Jessie.

Jessie hit the door and shoved her way past the crowd. As Sarah hit the door, she heard the kitten from inside the pocket. She got it out and held it close to her chest.

"My bus!" Jessie yelled.

The train whistle sounded.

"Stop!" Sarah screamed.

Jessie had run past Bick's burning shop and house. She was rounding the corner to go back around where the wrecking yard was. Back behind to find her bus.

Sarah was shoving herself past the crowd, finally seeing what was happening. She saw Jessie as she disappeared. "Stop!"

From the other end of town, she heard a roar of an engine. Everybody turned to see what the noise was. It was the ranger's SUV. Sarah started to run to where Jessie was. The bartender grabbed her arm and said, "No!"

"Let me go!"

"Can't."

She elbowed him, still holding the kitten. "Let me go!"

The man that had harassed them earlier grabbed her from behind and said into her ear, "Calm down, Sarah. You get to stay with us. We can't have you get hurt in that fire. Featus would never forgive us." He laughed.

The ranger sped past them to the junkyard.

Jessie was running back to the crowd when the ranger put his vehicle in reverse and cut Jessie off. She tried to run around the other way. The ranger jumped out and grabbed her. She struggled to get away, but it was no use. She was no match for the ranger. He carried her to the driver's side door. She was fighting all the way. He shoved her inside, and as he did she hit the gearshift into drive and mashed on the gas. It spun out, with the ranger holding on to the door and door frame. It was dragging him for a bit before he could pull himself inside. They were halfway across town by the time he was behind the wheel. He hit Jessie so hard in the face it knocked her out cold.

Sarah was still fighting to get away. She was yelling and kicking as the SUV started rolling. They let Sarah go at that point. She took off after it but could not catch it. She fell to the ground, still holding the kitten tight, and began to cry.

Thunder! Very loud, it began to pour down rain. It was sheets of water flooding the town.

Sarah took off to J.R.'s store. The day was coming very fast. The ground was actually shaking. She was drenched; she threw the door open and ran inside. She locked the door and went down the aisle toward the house. She was halfway down when the kitten began to meow hysterically and jumped from her arms. The kitten was back at the front door meowing and pawing at the door, frantically. She turned and ran to the kitten.

The train whistle sounded.

As she approached the door, she saw a car. It was the same one that had picked J.R. up the night before. It stopped in front of the store on the other side of the street. Sarah could not see the driver. What she did see was J.R. get out of the passenger's side, look at her for a split-second, then look behind them. He got back in, slammed the door, and they took off toward what used to be Bick's shop.

Sarah was fumbling with the lock, trying to get it to unlock. She did it. She stepped outside and watched. The automobile with J.R. in it flipped around right in front the smoldering building. When suddenly Sarah heard an engine sound coming from the other way. The sound raced closer. The ranger's SUV rumbling toward her, past the graveyard and roared on.

"Oh no!" Sarah screamed. It was a game of chicken, right before her eyes. The car didn't swerve! It was the ranger that turned his steering wheel to the right! Right then, Sarah's question about the mail was answered. No, they did not pick up the mail here in Bellowing Hollers. There were envelopes flying all over the instant the Ranger ran into the box. The box flipped over his vehicle; letters scattered.

Sarah was racing on foot after the car. She was at the beginning of the graveyard when the ranger swung his vehicle around to face the graveyard. He recklessly went around Sarah and slammed on his brakes in front of her. The car was out of sight.

The rain and thunder had stopped.

The new overseer jumped out of the passenger side and ran after Sarah. He seized her. He had his arms around her waist. She was fighting to get away when the ranger walked up, laughing hysterically.

The ranger asked Sarah with a nonchalant attitude, "Did you meet Richard, Richard Flower? He's the one holding you." He was amusing himself.

Richard pushed Sarah to the ranger. She tried to run, but the ranger caught her. He licked her face and shoved her back to Richard. Richard trapped her; he was chuckling. "You are right about this one's looks. She's sweet!"

Sarah heard the loud meow over by the store. Still fighting, she quickly glanced and there stood Featus, eyes glowing crimson. She looked back at the ranger, his face suddenly changing to serious when he noticed Featus.

"Let me go!" screamed Sarah.

Richard was still laughing and hanging onto Sarah when the ranger bellowed, "You heard Sarah, Richard, let her go. Now!"

Confused, Richard shoved her over to the Ranger. He caught her and asked in a sugar-coated voice, "Are you all right, Sarah?"

Sarah pushed away from the ranger. "Screw you!" She noticed the kitten just two feet away from Featus. Fearing for the kitten's life, she tried to keep Featus's attention on her. As she neared Featus, she heard a shrill screech from behind her. It was Richard; the ranger was kicking and hitting him, beating him. "How dare you disrespect Sarah like that! You will not have what was promised to you now. You will pay for treating that special girl the way you did!" Richard was lying on the ground barely moving, with the energy he had left, trying to block the kicks.

"Thank you for saving me, Featus." She handed him her necklace with the four-leaf clover attached.

Featus smiled as he took it and said, "Sarraah," in his soft, eerie voice.

The ranger was now dragging Richard to the store. "Since we can't trust you, you will run the store then. Get in there, you shit!" as he shoved Richard through the door.

Featus held his hand out for Sarah. "Sarah."

Sarah took his hand in hers. They walked along the side of the store, the graveyard on the other side. Back behind, they walked. As they got to the end of the store, Sarah heard the sound of an engine starting up, she turned quickly. It was only the ranger. Turning back looking at Featus, he was staring up at her. His eyes were not that violent red, but a calming hazel. He led her along a path away from the store.

Before they entered the trees, Sarah looked back. There were black clouds, not only hovering over, but also covering all of Bellowing Hollers. She turned and walked into the trees. It was a short walk through the trees. The bright light hurt her eyes. She had not seen the sun in four days. She glimpsed back, and all she could see were trees.

They continued on, around a corner, over a bridge, and there it was. It looked like a fairytale house. Almost picture-perfect. There was a driveway leading up to what appeared to be the garage, with flowers on each side of the driveway. The house even had a white picket fence surrounding the property. Green shutters. This is the house she had always dreamed of, although much bigger.

"Is this your house, Featus? Do your parents live here?"

Featus's eyes blackened with a tint of red. Sarah, seeing this, became frightened. He gripped her hand tighter and began to walk up the drive again. She got a sick feeling in her stomach and stopped suddenly. "I want to go back!" she yanked her hand from his.

"Sarah, come in," Featus said, in a soft, still voice.

The train whistle sounded.

CHAPTER 30

Déjà vu
(For Real)

Sarah heard a kitten meow and a striking sound. Jessie was screaming out in fear, "Sarah!" The kitten meowed, another strike, "Sarah, wake up!" "Meow."

"Give me the candle, Sarah!"

Sarah reached blindly in what little light the match let out. She found it with no problem and handed it to Jessie. She got another candle, lit it, and placed it on the dresser. And then did the same with another.

Jessie searched for the kitten. There were fuzzy balls all over the bed; tossing them off, she continued searching radically for the kitten. In her haste, she glanced quickly to the corner of the room where there was no light, she saw the red glowing eyes that looked the same as the ones they had seen the night they were camping. The night that Steve had died . . . She looked away hastily. She rubbed her chin and felt blood!

"Did the kitten bite you?"

"I don't know."

"Meow."

"It *was* the kitten, Sarah!"

"Meow," the kitten was pounding toward Jessie from the end of the bed. Jessie reached for it. "Meow," there was a little blood around the kitten's mouth. Jessie held it close to her heart.

Sarah was searching for more of the fuzzy things and slapping them off the bed. She continued lighting all of the candles.

"Shit, Sarah, we almost died in our sleep, and this kitten saved us."

"That was the worst dream . . . well, actually it wasn't."

"No doubt, man. We've got to go, Sarah."

"I wonder what . . . time it . . . is?" Sarah asked.

Jessie got up, ready to go. Sarah was ready and waiting. "Déjà vu," Sarah said.

"What?" Jessie put the kitten in her jacket pocket and its food in the other pocket.

"Nothing."

They walked down the hallway, opened the store door. Looking into the store, it was still dark . . . no J.R.

"He's gone," Jessie stated the obvious. "Let's go to the Froth and see if anybody saw anything—like who did J.R. leave with." They exited the store.

Walking to the other end of town, Sarah said, "I wonder if they ever pick up the mail . . ." She drifted off. Oh shit, in her mind she was standing there with Featus in front of a big white house, with a long driveway.

"Sarah!" Jessie was saying, shaking her. "What is it, man? Are you OK?"

"We did this before," Sarah said, still staring off into space.

"What are you talking about?"

"Everything up to this point, we've done already."

"You're getting way out there, Sarah."

"No! Listen to me, Jessie. From the time we woke up, or should I say, you woke up and screamed at me to wake up. The kitten biting your chin, to when I said that about the mailbox, *we did it already*, and I know what's going to happen next!"

"What?"

"We're going to the Grease Trap to eat, and it'll be closed."

Shaking her head and looking at Sarah as though she had lost her mind, Jessie said, "I bet they don't pick up the mail. Let's go across the street and check it out."

Sarah grabbed Jessie's arm and bawled, "Listen to me! We did this! We've got to change it! Even if it were just a dream, everything is happening again!"

"I'm thinking we should take off right after we eat and find out anything about J.R. or anything at all."

"Damn it, Jessie! We won't eat. The Grease Trap *will be closed.* There will be a man talking to the bartender. As we walk in, the bartender will say to him, 'pay up.'"

Jessie started to say something, when Sarah shushed her. "Listen to me! And don't talk. I don't want you to say a word until we go to the bathroom at the Froth. Promise me, Jessie!"

"You are losing it, Sarah!"

"No, I'm not! Promise me, you won't talk or even think about your VeeDub either!"

"I was thinking after we eat, we could go . . ."

"Shut up, Jessie! Don't say it! There will be a fire, and the ranger will take you! Please believe me and then we can make some sort of plan. Please, Jessie! Please!"

Jessie was looking at Sarah like she had totally lost it now. But she agreed.

They walked down to the Grease Trap, the sign read . . . **CLOSED**. "No way," Jessie said. "It can't be two already. We slept . . ."

"Yeah, we slept that late! I asked you not to talk, and you agreed! Please, just trust me!"

"OK!" Jessie shot back.

Sarah continued, "We'll go to the Froth. Don't mention anything about your bus or Bick's place!"

"But Sarah, I was thinking . . ."

"No! Pay attention, this is what's going to happen. When it happens, will you believe me then?"

"I believe you now."

"This is what's going to happen. We'll walk in, there will be a man. His name is Richard Flower. The bartender will say to him 'pay up!' They made a bet about us. Richard is a smart-ass. You *must* ignore him."

They got to the Froth and stopped at the door. "We'll go to the bathroom and make a plan."

"Sarah, you're really freakin' me out, man. If this happens like you say, I'll really be wiggin' then!"

"I know, but we can change things because I do know. But you must listen to me! We'll change things in the bathroom. OK?"

"Yeah, OK Sarah."

They walked in.

"Pay up."

The man sitting at the bar turned and looked at the girls, turned back, took his wallet out and handed the bartender some money.

"Thank you," said the bartender as he put the money in his front pocket.

"Thanks to you girls, I just lost fifty dollars."

"Screw you, Dick weed!" Jessie shouted at the man who lost the bet.

Sarah grabbed Jessie's arm and dragged her to the restroom.

"Dick weed?" the bartender laughed. "She really knows your name, Richard!"

"Maybe we just changed it," Sarah whispered.

They were almost to the restroom when the bartender hollered, "I think the phone line is up," holding the phone to his ear.

They turned and hurriedly walked back to the bar.

"Can I use your phone?" Sarah asked.

The bartender hung up the phone as they approached. "I knew you girls were still with us, and Richard here said you girls were gone. Hey, Jessie, what happened to your chin?"

Jessie turned to Richard and snapped, "How would we leave, asshole?"

As they approached the bar, Sarah asked, "Will you hand me the phone, please?"

Walking toward the front door, Richard turned around and said, "I didn't say you left, I said you were gone." Richard laughed as he turned back around and continued walking to the door.

"Go to hell!" Jessie roared.

"Jessie, Stop!" Sarah screamed.

"Ladies seem to go first around here, Jessie!" Richard shot back as the door closed behind him.

"The phone, please," Sarah asked.

The bartender picked up the phone, put it to his ear, and set the receiver back down again. "I guess it went down again." He shrugged.

A lady got up from behind them and walked to the restroom.

Sarah grabbed Jessie by the jacket and pulled her to the restroom. They pushed their way through the door.

Before it closed, the bartender yelled, "When the ranger finds out J.R. is gone, shit's really going to hit the fan."

Sarah stopped in her tracks. Still holding the door open, she said to Jessie, "Why don't you say something now?"

Looking at the bartender, Jessie shrugged and said, "I don't know."

The door closed. The same lady that met them in the restroom the last time handed Jessie a note.

Sarah snatched the note from Jessie, crumpled it up and swallowed it. "We're going to change this!" She said, almost crying. "We know all about this!"

The lady turned to exit.

Jessie asked, "How do you know who to trust?"

Sarah screamed, "Noo!"

Before the lady went out, she said, "Go with your first instincts." The door closed behind her.

"Shit!" Jessie yelled.

"No, Jessie! Every time it starts to change, something is said like it happened before. You're not listening to me." Sarah cried. "We have to change this! I am going to change it now! This is what's going to happen." She told Jessie what she dreamed and what they should do. "What do you think?"

"Sounds good, if it's like you said."

"It will be. Let's go."

"Before we go, I need to use the go," Jessie said.

They walked out. Jessie opened her mouth to say something. Sarah interrupted, "Just like I said, right?" She grabbed Jessie's arm, "Come this way." They went to the bar where the phone was kept.

Jessie, taking off her jacket as they approached the bar, said, "What in the hell is going on? I see the flames, but why are all the people just standing out there?"

Sarah picked up the phone. It rang.

The whistle sounded.

She heard a voice saying, "I'm on my way." Sarah's eyes widened. She dropped the receiver and said, "It sounds like . . ."

The kitten jumped from Jessie's pocket and ran toward the front door. Jessie took off after it. At the moment the kitten reached the door, the lady from the restroom opened it and called to them, "You girls should see this, it's bad!"

The kitten ran out. "Jessie! No! Stop!"

"The whistle scared the kitten. Let's go this way, Sarah!"

"No, let's go out the back like we planned!"

"I can't leave the cat! Let's go through the alley!" Jessie took off out the door.

Sarah followed. The crowd was busy watching the fire and was not paying attention to them. They rounded the corner to enter the alley. There stood Richard Flower. Jessie ran into him; Sarah ran into Jessie. He smiled. "The kitten ran down the alley. I do believe Featus hunted a new pet. Well, you know how fast that little shit can be." He laughed.

"Move out of our way!" Jessie demanded.

As this was happening, Sarah noticed all of the townspeople turn to watch them. They started linking elbows and making a circle around the trio. She grabbed Jessie by the collar and whispered in her ear, "Let's go the other way, and we need to run. Now!" They turned to run. As they did this, the crowd circled tighter. Sarah turned to the lady they had just met in the restroom, "Let us pass, please!"

The lady responded, "They promised us a trade. If you girls will just go with them and help them, they can complete their mission and our town will be freed."

"It's a lie! Let us go!" Sarah rammed into them. They didn't budge. Jessie rammed a different spot. No luck there either. Sarah spoke out, "Don't believe what they say! They won't free you! We must unite!"

Richard grabbed each of their arms, "Girls . . ."

They heard the roar of an engine. "We are so sorry!" Sarah heard one of the crowd say.

"Then help us, let us go!"

The ranger's vehicle stopped. A door opened then closed. Richard turned to Sarah and grabbed her by the waist. She was fighting to get away as the Ranger was walking up. Jessie was also fighting him to free Sarah. The ranger walked up.

"I see you've already met Richard Flower." Richard pushed Sarah to the ranger. She tried to get away, but the ranger grabbed her. Jessie was yelling and fighting the ranger now. He shoved Jessie. She hit the ground hard. After that he turned, smiled at Sarah, and licked her face. Then shoved her back to Richard.

Richard grabbed her; he was laughing too. He took hold of one of her arms. "You are right about this one's looks. She's sweet." And then he whispered in her ear, "Don't think freaky Featus will come to your rescue, Sarah! That only happens in dreams." He laughed hysterically.

Sarah and Jessie heard a meow by the other end of the building.

That was when everything changed.

They knocked Sarah and Jessie out with chloroform . . .

CHAPTER 31

Nothing's Changed

The ranger tied the girls with tie wraps and put them in the back of his SUV. Before he departed, he stood in front of the crowd and told them, "You not only did the right thing, but you did exactly what was expected. The masters do appreciate the cooperation you have given to me and to your new overseer. I . . . no . . . we expect the same respect you had given to Daniel toward Mr. Richard Flower."

Someone from the crowd yelled, "You said we would be freed of all this darkness . . ."

"As I was saying . . ." The kitten ran along the building, past the crowd. Richard tried to kick her but missed. She stopped at the next building, which was the Grease Trap, and stared at the ranger's vehicle for a few seconds. She looked back at the ranger and Richard, then she hissed. She turned and ran toward the other end of town. The ranger continued, telling the townspeople, "Everything will remain the same as it has been for the past . . ." He thought about it for a few seconds. "Close to eight years now. I will let you know through Richard when everything is completed and functioning. The final stages are in the back of my truck, as I speak. Go about your business." He turned to walk to his SUV then turned back. "Oh yes, and one more thing." Everybody turned back to the ranger. "Daniel . . . when he recovers, a bit more that is, will be the new storekeeper. It will reopen within a few days, I'm sure. And you can pay your final respects to J.R., just look for the newest headstone. Good evening!"

He turned, got in, and drove off down past the town and past the graveyard.

Most of the people went inside the Froth Finder. The others stayed outside to talk and watch the building burn.

CHAPTER 32

Clean Room

Jessie sat straight up and gasped. Everything was white and silver. *Stainless steel, just like the bathroom at the Froth.* It smelled like a hospital. She looked around, mind running rampant. *This must be a dream. It's unreal. This can't be happening!* There are bars on the window. She looked under the sheet that was covering her. She had nothing on. *Naked?* "What is going on here?" she demanded. "It's got to be a dream!" she said out loud. Silence. *Was I hurt in an accident?* She wiggled her toes and fingers. Shook her legs and arms. *I feel fine. Why am I in a hospital . . . no . . . not a hospital or there wouldn't be bars on the window. It's gotta be a dream, yes, a dream.* She looked around for a button to call for a nurse. *No button. If this is a dream, I would dream a button to call someone. Wouldn't I?* There was what looked to be an operating table in the middle of the room. "What am I doing here?" *Why is there an operating table in here? Bars on the window? Am I in a mental hospital?* she thought, *Did I end up like mom, after all? Why is the floor stainless steel? And the walls?* The ceiling was the regular dropped ceiling, insulated with two-by-four-foot panels. *Have I gone nuts?* She sat up, legs hanging over the side of the bed. *What am I doing here!* "Help me!"

—————

Sarah had awakened. She sat straight up, looking around, rubbing her head with both hands. *My head aches, what happened to me?*

Where am I? The smell of alcohol nauseated her. Everything in her room was white. *There are bars on the window.* She thought. *Why? And why am I in this hospital?* She began looking around for a button to call a nurse or a doctor. There wasn't one. "Hello, is anybody here?" she yelled. She thought she heard a faint cry. *Sarah.* It was muffled, or was that her imagination? *Where am I? What a terrible nightmare, or was it? It seemed so real.* She stood, almost lost her balance. Rubbing her head, she walked to the door. *Locked.* "Jessie!" *Did somebody just scream "help me?"* Pounding on the door with her fist, she wailed, "Let me out! Somebody, anybody, let me out of here!"

———⧾∿∽⧸⧹∾⧼∿∿———

Jessie heard stifled cries but really couldn't make out who or what it was. She heard banging, but it was also muffled. She got up, ripped the sheet off the bed, wrapped it around herself, and headed for the door. *Feels like someone hit me over the head.* She tried the doorknob. *Damn it, it's locked.* She kicked the door twice then listened. There was more banging. It sounded like it was coming from the room next to hers. She went to the wall where the sound was coming from and slammed it with her fist. That accomplished nothing but to hurt her hand. *Hitting the door is louder.* She went back to the door and kicked it four times. Glancing back behind her, she saw the operating table. This put a new fear inside of her, and she began to hit the door with her fists. She bawled out, "Sarah! Sarah! Somebody let me out of here!"

———⧾∿∽⧸⧹∾⧼∿∿———

Tears running down Sarah's face, she cried out, "Jessie, Where are you? Knock once if you can hear me." Nothing. She put her forehead against the door and sobbed. She felt as though someone had split her head in half with an axe. With her head still resting against the cool steel of the door, she whimpered, "Let me out. Please, oh God, please help me. Let me out."

The banging stopped. Jessie, holding her head between her hands, knelt down, back against the wall and whimpered.

A booming voice came over a speaker. The speaker was mounted in the ceiling. *Just like the hospital,* Jessie thought.

"Good day, ladies. We are going to need for you to calm down." The voice was very calming. "We are going to need for you to go back to your beds and lie down and just relax. I will be in to welcome you ladies in an hour or so. In the meantime, you must take it easy."

"What's going on here? Where are my clothes?" shrieked Jessie.

"Jessie, we can see you but cannot hear you."

Both Sarah and Jessie looked rapidly around the room for a camera. Nothing.

"Ladies." Then came a soothing laugh. "You won't be able to see the cameras. What is important is that we can see you. Now go and rest peacefully, and as I said, I will be in to introduce myself in a short while. I will then answer any questions you girls may have."

"Why is there an operating table in here?" bellowed Jessie.

"Like I said before, Jessie, I cannot hear you. And neither can anyone else, for that matter."

Jessie flipped the bird with both hands, held them over her head and turned a complete circle. "Can you see this, asshole?"

There was no response.

CHAPTER 33

You're the Lucky One

Sarah heard tapping from the middle of the wall on the other side of the room. This was not as muted. She went to her bed, sat down, and tapped back. She put her ear against the wall and heard, "Hear me . . . hello. Can you hear me?"

"Yes," Sarah said into cupped hands, touching the wall. And then she turned her ear back to the wall to listen.

"Cover your head with your sheets so they can't see you."

After doing so, Sarah responded, "It's covered. Who are you?"

"Find something, like a cup out of the bathroom, so you can hear me better and I can hear you. Tap twice if you understand."

Tap tap . . .

She got up and went to the door that read "Restroom." It was on the opposite side of the room that her bed was on. She tried to open it, it was locked. She kicked the door.

"You may now enter the restroom."

Sarah heard a click and opened the door. She went inside. There was another door on the other side of the room. She tried to open it. *Locked.* She used the toilet. She finished and was washing her hands. While the water was running, she thought she heard the sound of the doorknob rattling. She turned the water off quickly. Silence. She took one of the cups and hid it under her gown. As the door clicked closed, she stopped. *Was that the other door in there, opening and closing?* She stopped to listen and could not hear anything. She went back to her bed and covered her head with the sheet. She put her cup next to the wall and her ear to the cup.

Tap tap.

"Can you hear me better?"

"A little," Sarah answered.

"That's good. Now we won't have to talk so loud. They can hear in your room, no matter what they say."

"That's good to know. Where are we?" Sarah said into the cup, then turned the cup back over and placed her ear to it again.

"Are there two of you? There are always two at a time."

"Yes, but I think Jessie's in the room next to mine. But I'm not totally sure."

"That's the operating room. She'll be first. You're the lucky one."

"What are you talking about?" Sarah questioned.

The girl started to say something, then stopped and said, "They're here . . ."

It was silent after that. Sarah kept the cup to the wall, trying to listen. All she could hear were murmurs.

CHAPTER 34

Lifesaver

Jessie went over and tried to open the restroom door. "The restroom is occupied. Please be patient."

Jessie turned toward the window and looked out. *It's daylight! I can actually see daylight! Trees and green grass.* She opened the window and took a deep breath. *Fresh air and blue sky!* She shook the bars on the window. *Damn! No way, they won't budge.* She took another deep breath. *This fresh air is great!* She took in another deep breath. That was when she noticed a small gray thing bouncing through the field, getting closer to the house. *Little fur ball. Could that be? Maybe . . .* She closed the window and moved away from it. *Just in case they're watching me. I don't want to endanger my LS, short for lifesaver.* She thought. *Oh shit, I'm turning into J.R. She laughed out loud and said,* "Or my mother!" She laughed louder.

Jessie turned, facing the operating table, and got a sick feeling in her stomach. She decided to snoop!

CHAPTER 35

Our Rescuer

Sarah, head still under the sheet and ear to the wall, said to herself, "Damn!" *Can't hear a thing! Oh man. They're coming. Who's they? Are they coming here next?* Sarah hid the cup under her pillow and went to the window. She opened it. As she did, she heard another window closing. "Jessie?" she said, almost in a yell. She did not want anybody to hear her. She listened for a minute. And heard nothing! She looked out the window and saw a small gray *kitten* jumping through the field. *Our rescuer!* Sarah laughed quietly and closed the window. She did not want to draw attention to it. She looked around, then decided to go back and wait for her neighbor to tap on the wall again.

Tap tap . . .

CHAPTER 36

Thought Transference

Jessie was going over every inch of the room. All the drawers and cabinets, *empty!* Just then the main door opened, and in walked a man, a doctor. He was wearing a white robe and had a stethoscope around his neck.

She walked over toward him, straightening the sheets as she was yelling, "Just what in the hell is this? Are we prisoners here, or what? Where is Sarah? Where are my clothes?"

As she got closer, he told her, "Stop, Jessie, listen to me, please."

"Why should I?" Jessie burst out.

"I am not the cause. Please understand. I, I . . ."

"*Who is the cause?* Why don't you get *that* asshole in here!"

"No, you do not want that. Please, listen to me and I, uh, you can understand. Please," the doctor said, with his hands trembling. "You, you must . . ."

"Why am I trapped here? *Doctor!*"

"Calm down, please. And . . . and listen . . ."

"Who took my clothes? Doctor!"

"Please you, uh, I, uh . . . we don't want the Masters to come. Please, let me talk. Please, Jessie. All will be explained. I don't want to paralyze you in order to fill you in, please."

"*Paralyze* me, doctor! What do you mean?"

"Please . . . please, let me explain," the doctor said, moving toward the bed. "Come sit, please, Jessie."

"What in the hell are you talking about, Doctor! Paralyze *me* to fill me *in?*"

"Yes . . . uh no . . . uh, please listen." He was shaking very hard now. "Jessie, uh, please, Sarah is with us too, you know. Please, listen to me."

Jessie was walking back to the bed from the door the doctor just entered through. She spotted the kitten on the window ledge. She calmed down, not wanting the doctor to see LS. "What? You have three minutes!"

"OK." The doctor patted the bed next to him. "Please, come . . ."

"Quit with the *please*, Doctor Shithead!"

"OK, OK, you are here of your own free will . . ."

"That's B.S., doctor shithead!"

"No . . . I mean plea—, no listen, it started with the preacher, right? I mean, he said for you not to come, please . . . I mean, first you must understand that."

"*No bullshit!* We are captured! Simply! We want to leave, and you guys won't let us! You must understand that!"

"Oh, this is not going well at all!" the doctor said, rubbing his face with his shaking hands. "OK, OK, listen . . . if you will not let me explain, it will be worse for you girls. Let me think for a minute. Sit, please." He patted the bed once more.

"*No.* I choose not to *sit*, Doctor!" Jessie snuck a quick look at LS curled up on the window ledge, staring into her eyes. "Just tell me why we're here! Where my clothes are, and what do we have to do to leave this prison!" She thought, *Go find Sarah!* The kitten jumped down and was gone.

At that moment, the doctor turned quickly to look at the window, "Uh, what?"

"What, what?"

"Uh, yes, Sarah is with us, we do not have to find her."

Dr. Shithead can read minds, or what? What am I thinking, you scumbag! Tell me! "OK, Sarah is here? Where? And what are we doing here?"

"OK, listen now. You girls have been chosen."

The kitten reappeared. Jessie glanced quickly at her. *Sarah is in the next room.*

"Yes. Sarah is in the next room. Uh, as I was saying, you have been chosen for a very, very, important, uh . . . mission. Yes . . ." The doctor tried to sound convincing.

Go and come back later, Jessie thought, glancing at the kitten. *Back in a while* shot back in Jessie's mind.

"OK, uh, I will come back in a while." The doctor started to stand.

"No! What mission are you talking about?"

"I cannot disclose that information as of yet."

"What can you tell me, *Doctor*? Chosen for what, Doctor?"

"Well, you see . . . uh, you both are very, very young and very, very healthy . . ."

"OK, *Doctor* Shithead . . ."

"Oh please, I mean, call me Dr. Plubblix."

"I think Doctor Shithead is more appropriate, but if you insist, Dr. Pubic! Who, in this godforsaken place, took my clothes?"

"When you were brought here, the masters examined you to make sure you had no flaws. And well, you are one of the chosen ones!" he said, beaming.

"The chosen *what*? And who took my clothes?"

"The chosen . . . *ones*," the doctor said with a smile. "Your clothes . . . why yes . . ."

"Get out, Doctor Pube! You aren't answering a damn thing! Just get out and send someone that knows their head from their ass!"

"But I do—"

"Out!"

CHAPTER 37

Queen Mother

Tap tap . . .

Sarah put the cup up to the wall again and her ear up to the cup. She heard, "Are you there?"

Sarah answered, "Yes, I'm here. What happened?"

"The doctor came in to examine me. He said the transplant must happen very soon."

"What transplant?"

"The doctor will explain everything. You are truly the lucky one."

"What are you talking about?"

"You will be the Queen Mother of the future. I so hoped it would be me. My mother sacrificed herself, in the hope that I would be the Queen Mother and go down in history as so," said the voice in the other room.

"I'm not understanding. I hope . . ." Sarah said, drifting off.

The kitten had come to her window and curled up in the corner of the window's ledge. She was staring at the main door in Sarah's room. Sarah had taken the cup away from the wall and just held it, staring at the kitten, trying to digest everything the girl had said. Suddenly the click of the door opening startled her. *Go!* she thought to the kitten. She darted off.

The door opened; in walked a man dressed as a doctor. "Uh, please, I, um, will go after I s-speak to you a b-bit, uh, Sarah."

"Why am I here?" demanded Sarah.

"Well, you see," the doctor was saying as he walked toward Sarah. "I, uh, we, appreciate you and Jessie volunteering . . ."

"Stop right there! I—no, we never volunteered for shit!"

"Oh dear, please calm, I can explain," he was saying in a nervous voice, hands shaking. "Please sit, uh . . ." He noticed the cup that Sarah was holding. His demeanor changed instantly. "What are you doing with a cup in here?" he asked, with venom in his voice.

"I was thirsty, so I brought it out of the bathroom."

"Well," the doctor said, looking up at the corner between the restroom and window. His eyes shone a glint of red around his irises as he waved his right arm.

The train whistle sounded.

"As I was saying, you girls came here of your own free will."

"No! That's bullshit!"

The doctor changed back to the unsteady little guy he was when he first walked in. Even his hands had begun to quiver again. His eyes were back to normal. "Oh, I mean. Please, oh my, not this again" the doctor shivered.

"Just answer my question! Why am I here?"

The door opened. In walked Richard Flower. "Doctor?" he bowed his head to the doctor.

"Cup," the doctor said and pointed quickly at the cup Sarah was holding.

Richard walked over to Sarah. Sarah recoiled. "Get that jerk away from me!"

Richard stopped and laughed a phony *ha ha ha.*

The doctor walked over to Sarah with his hand held out and said, "Cup." Sarah handed the cup to the doctor. He handed it to Richard and demanded, "Paper!" Richard turned and walked out.

The doctor went over and sat on the bed, facing the door. He patted the bed with his trembling hand and sniveled. "Please, Sarah. Please." She went over to him, facing him and the window, stood there in front of him.

The kitten jumped up on the window's ledge and curled up, staring at Sarah. She heard in her mind, "*Calm.*"

"Oh yes, I am calming. Thank you." The doctor drew in a deep breath. "OK, I am better now."

Sarah, looking puzzled at the doctor's response, said, "OK, great." And she thought while looking at the kitten, "*Why are you here?*"

The doctor answered with a question. "Oh yes, I am here, uh, do you mean here in this room or here on this plan—um, in this town?" Spontaneously, the doctor turned to look out the window. The split-second before he did so, the kitten had jumped down. "As I was saying, it's a privilege, and I do appreciate your freewillingness . . . is that a word? Freewillingness, hum. I rather like it, actually . . ."

"Why are we here?" Sarah demanded.

The main door opened, and in walked Richard with a stack of paper cups. He went directly to the restroom door. He stood in front of the door, staring up at the corner until the door clicked. He opened it and went inside. He stayed in there for a few seconds. On the way out, he nodded once at the doctor and then exited.

The doctor watched Richard. After the door closed behind Richard, the doctor turned back to Sarah and said, "You *are* the chosen one, Sarah!"

"What are you going to do with *us*? Can you at least answer that?"

"We, uh, yes. I can. Please be calm, OK Sarah? Let us start over. My name is Dr. Plubblix. I am the liaison between the masters and yourself. I will be the one preparing you girls for your destiny! You see?" He smiled widely.

"Go to hell! Get out of here, you freak!"

"Well, I see you may need a little more time to . . . well, gain some understanding." The doctor got up and walked to the main door. Reaching for the doorknob, he stopped and turned back to look at Sarah, his eyes glowing bright red. "Twenty-four hours! I will be back! You girls better not irritate me any further." He went out, and the door clicked locked.

CHAPTER 38

Neighbors

The kitten was hopping back across the field. Jessie watched with the window open, appreciating the fresh air.

After the doctor left Sarah's room, Sarah went to the window and opened it. She watched the kitten going back to the woods through the field. She stood there trying to put everything that she had learned in perspective. Everything from what the girl had told her, to what the doctor didn't tell her. *Oh man, why?* She saw a bird flying above the kitten. *No, a hawk!* Getting ready to swoop down on the kitten! "*Run!*" she screamed.

"Sarah, is that you?"

"Jessie?"

"What . . ." Jessie started but could not be heard over the train whistle that had just begun to shriek. The piercing noise was continuous. They could not hear one another. Jessie slammed the window down. The whistle stopped. She saw the kitten had made it to the edge of the woods before she started pounding on the wall that separated her and Sarah. "Sarah!" she shrieked.

Sarah slammed her window down as well. She began to pace around the room. Her ears still ringing, and she could hear the stifled sounds of pounding from the room where Jessie was being held prisoner. Sarah kicked the same wall three times.

Jessie heard the barely audible kicks and then realized: *This is doing no good! I need a plan! We need a plan!*

CHAPTER 39

Compliance

While the two girls were being held on the second floor in separate rooms, there was a meeting going on in the basement, at the controls of the house. The meeting consisted of Doctor Plubblix, Richard Flower, the ranger, and Featus. Featus was pacing back and forth behind Richard and the ranger. That made both of them very nervous, especially Richard, who kept glancing back at Featus. The doctor sat behind a large desk with computers and monitors. They were monitoring each room of the house and various spots of the exterior surrounding the property. The doctor sat there, tapping his first two fingers on his lips, staring at the screens. His eyes were glowing a brilliant red. "This is not going well! You said Sarah and Jessie were ready and willing!" He said, still not looking away from the source of luminescent light that was bathing his face in blue glow.

The ranger's head bowed, looking up with his eyes at the doctor. He answered, "Master, I said that they came here to Bellowing Hollers of their own free will."

"You must know by now that for the procedure that will be performed, the subjects must be participating with some sort of enthusiasm. It took . . . damn near the whole town, trial and error, in order for Featus to be! Now, Heather has less than one week before the transplant *must* take place. It took four hosts for Featus! Now I am trying to do it with three. It should have the same outcome. Although I noticed quite a bit more pain and agony with this female and the last one, that's all right if it saves one. I do not think they feel

118

pain like we do, or should I say like *you* males do. Did you not say that is why females exist, to reproduce? Anyway, the creation is quite a bit larger and is impressively healthy. We are coming up on two years of development with . . ."

The speaker crackled to life with Jessie's voice, "Doctor Pubic! I have to pee! Can you get them to open this freakin' door, you prick! And bring me my clothes!"

Richard chuckled his three ha ha ha's. This would be the last thing Richard ever spoke.

Featus ran so fast, startling everyone in the room, and hit Richard's leg. This knocked him to his knees. Featus punched him twice in the ribs and then jumped on Richard's back. He wrapped his right arm around Richard's neck and his left arm around his shoulder. And then bit down on the vein protruding from Richard's neck. Featus stayed like that for at least five minutes. Richard Flower never made a sound.

In the meantime, the doctor had opened his door for Jessie. The doctor looked at the ranger, his eyes not glowing so vibrantly now, "Featus cannot stand a smart-ass laughing at his father, his creator, like that. Oh yes, and Featus conveyed to me that Richard's last coherent thought was 'that little shit,' referring to Featus." The doctor laughed somewhat. Sounding exhausted, eyes not glowing at all now, he said, rubbing his hands over his tired face, "We need . . . um, a new, um . . . overseer, n-now."

"They're getting hard to come by, Doctor."

"There's the, um, bartender. This should be the l-last, the uh, last one we'll need. T-tell him not to even think negativel . . . nega . . . um . . . badly toward anyone Featus cares for. I'm hoping it'll only take eleven m-months with J-Jessie. If it happens like I'm planning, we can . . . uh spare, you know. I believe we can keep a l-lid on this mountain for another year. D-don't you?" Not waiting for a response, "Oh never mind, you never thought this could be d-done. Anyway, after F-11 is, um . . . completed, we can make the move! L-Louisiana! That's where we'll really test the waters. I hate spending all the . . . uh, Homo sapiens for my own p-purpose, but it's really a requirement in order to save my spe . . . my, my, uhm. Do you understand?"

Featus finished and stood what was left of Richard up. Richard was pale, with a zombie look in his eyes. "I see you saved some for your quaydents. Night feeders, uh. Cute."

Featus nodded, with a wide smile.

"I do understand, Doctor, but I was wondering, what will you do with this town in the end?" the ranger asked, while keeping an eye on Featus. Featus seemed to grow before the ranger's eyes.

Featus was looking at the ranger, eyes glowing intense red.

The ranger took a step back.

The doctor quickly said, "Oh, uh, look at Sarah, she's at the, um, window."

"Sarah," Featus said in an adoring voice and then ran behind the desk to watch Sarah on the monitor.

Plubblix asked with a hint of crimson gleaming from his eyes. "Let me worry about that, Ranger. You will be going with us to Louisiana, won't you?"

The ranger answered, facing the floor, keeping an eye on Featus, "Well, of course, Master."

Plubblix continued, now in a weary voice, the glow no longer in his eyes, "To, you know, uh help us set up, and you know, set up shop there. And then you, uh . . . can do whatever you so choose."

"Oh yeah, sure."

Plubblix straightened up, shaking off any evidence of exhaustion and said, "But let us get back on track. Present time, present place. You *must* convince Jessie that she *will* make a perfect ending to a new beginning." He then added in a condescending voice, "Can you do that for us? Please? Tell me if you think that is too much to ask. Right now!"

Featus had stopped watching Sarah on the monitor, looked at the ranger, and was awaiting his answer.

"I will do it, Master!"

"I have noticed that Featus is feeding more often now. That is why it is so important for us to get to Louisiana. I believe it is there that we will finally have what is really required!" Changing his demeanor, slouching down, rubbing his face with shaky hands, Plubblix continued, "Oh my . . . I d-don't care for the uh, powder f-freaks, you know. That Featus loves the adr . . . uh, adrenaline, he really loves to get it going before he f-feeds. I just can't uh . . . acquire the taste for it, you know. Since Featus just uh . . . fed, you don't n-need to get him one . . . uh, tonight. I like, um, t-timid, you know." Sitting upright again, shoulders back, a hint of red around his irises, he commanded, "Be gone!"

The ranger turned to exit, still watching Featus.

"Oh, one more thing before you depart. You may want to bring Jessie some clothes to get her to cooperate with us!"

CHAPTER 40

Predestined

Jessie went into the restroom. While in there, she tried to open the other door leading into Sarah's room. While she was trying, a high-pitched, ear-piercing buzzer sounded. She let go quickly to cover her ears. She wondered if Sarah had heard it. She looked around. There was not much of anything. *Towels, soap, and paper cups.* She used the toilet. When finished, she went to wash her hands. *Oh man, it might work . . .*

Jessie exited the restroom and yelled, "I know you could hear me, you freaks! You're a bunch of idiots! Give me my clothes!"

———⚬⚬⚬⚬———

After kicking the wall, Sarah paced around for a while and then ended up staring out the window. *Where did the kitten go?* She wanted to open the window but feared the whistle would sound again if she did. She stood there, thinking, *How do I, or we, get out of this?* She heard a sound within the restroom. She grabbed the doorknob. The computer voice said, "The restroom is occupied, please be patient." Sarah released the knob, looked up at the corner where Richard had looked, and flipped the bird at it. She turned back to the window and stared out, looking out where the kitten had run. *Oh man!* She spotted movement out where the kitten had gone. *Did they see the cat and go after her? Are they hurting her?* She sighed. Walked back to her bed and tap tap tapped. Nothing.

CHAPTER 41

Blackness

After Jessie yelled she wanted her clothes, she went and plopped on the bed. *I hope Sarah gets the message.* All she could do is wait now. Suddenly, her door opened. It was the ranger. "Oh, shit!" she said, looking around for something to defend herself with. She got up, moving to the opposite side of the room, searching for something. There wasn't anything. Holding her bedsheet so it would not fall off her, she went to the other side of the operating table.

The ranger said in a very calm voice, "I am here as your preacher."

"No! You are no preacher! You are a sick and twisted bastard!"

"No, listen to me, Jessie. I am trying to warn you. Just like I tried to warn you before, remember?"

"Go to hell, Ranger!"

"This is about Sarah . . . and y-you."

"What did you do to Sarah?"

"I didn't do anything. Neither did *they* yet."

Jessie was glaring at the ranger.

"I brought you your clothes." He tossed them on the bed. "If you don't agree to do this, they will put the squeeze on Sarah. You know she's weaker than you and will agree to do it to save you. But it won't save you, though."

"What!"

"Just hear me out. They killed Richard just about fifteen minutes ago. And they will kill you too. You will have a greater chance of living if you agree to do the deal. You can agree to do this and it will spare Sarah, or not. She'll agree to do it to spare you. But it won't spare you. You'll be Featus's food!"

"Listen, I know you have no reason to trust me or believe me, but . . ." He stood there with his arms outstretched and hands open toward her.

"Agreeing to what? What are you talking about, man?"

"The doctor explained, didn't he?"

"Not a damn thing! He was talking around in circles, like you are!"

"He was supposed to be direct with you girls. Damn it!" the ranger said, emphasizing by hitting his fist against his open palm. "I always have to be the one, shit!"

"Doctor Pubic is a babbling idiot!"

"I'll tell you something," the ranger said, in a quiet voice, looking around. "I don't want to say it too loud." He moved closer to Jessie. "That's what got Richard killed. When you said, 'Doctor Pubic, open the door.'" He chuckled quietly.

"What are you saying?"

"You killed Richard and didn't even know it. You see, Richard laughed and they didn't appreciate it."

"So they killed him?"

"Yes, ma'am, Featus food! You're pretty funny, and they have no sense of humor."

"So just what is it I would be agreeing to do, Ranger?"

"Come closer. I'm not going to do anything. I'm just not sure what I am supposed to tell you."

"Let me get dressed first," she said as she was picking up her clothes from the bed, and she walked to the restroom. Before she entered, she spied LS hopping back across the field toward their prison. She hurried into the restroom, put her clothes on, and was back out within thirty seconds. She did not want the kitten to jump on the window ledge and for the ranger to see her. She rushed by the window, not risking even a glance out.

The ranger was now sitting on the operating table.

"What is that you're sitting on, an operating table?" Jessie inquired.

"This is an operating table, yes. Come closer, I won't do anything to you. You have my word. I just don't want to talk too loud." Then he barely said, "The walls have ears, if you know what I mean."

Jessie moved in closer, keeping her view of the window open. Drawing the ranger's sight away from the window so that even with his peripheral vision, he would not detect movement. "I figured that out! Why can't I talk to Sarah? And what's that operating table for?"

The kitten jumped up on the ledge and stared into Jessie's eyes.

"They will let you talk to Sarah once you have agreed to do this thing. The operating table, well . . . they will wheel in another table with a patient named Heather. She is with child. There will be a transplant. Heather is at her limit. She has a little more time but not much. You will be the third term, if you agree to it," whispered the ranger.

"Just what are you talking about?"

Jessie heard a voice in her head, *He's telling the truth.*

"Yes, I am telling the truth. It should be the third and final, the ranger was saying, as he cast his eyes down, staring at the floor.

Think black Jessie caught herself thinking.

"Yes, it is blackness, Jessie. But we really don't have a choice now, do we?"

Jessie began to think *Black, black, black . . .* until all she saw was black within her brain. "No, we don't—I guess," Jessie said, still seeing black in her mind.

I'm a conduit. As long as there are two humans and me, I can transfer thoughts from one to another. But you must see black in your head, or they can pick up on the images. Jessie knew now why she heard voices and understood that she was not going crazy after all. *All animals have, or what I mean is, all animals had this power in Bellowing Hollers. Which by the way was not the town's name eight years ago. It was Notrom. It was just a quaint little town with normal small-town problems. I didn't know I was capable of this when we were together in town. I met a crazy*— The kitten suddenly jumped down.

The ranger noticed Jessie gazing out the window and spun around rapidly to see what she was looking at. He saw nothing. Then realized all of this was probably overwhelming her, and she needed time to digest it all. "Are you OK?"

"Not really. Do I need to give you an answer now or can I see Sarah first?"

"I'll check with the masters. You rest and try to comprehend everything. I'll be back in an hour or so with your supper and an answer about Sarah." He stood and started for the door. He stopped and turned to face Jessie again. "It's really kind of sad, Jessie. You don't have much of a choice, and I am sorry for that. I'll be back." He hung his head down and exited.

Jessie went and sat on her bed, staring out the window. *Think* she thought to herself. *Think, think, think black!*

CHAPTER 42

Dead of Night Rendezvous

Sarah tapped on the wall on and off. She heard no response back. She wanted more information from the girl in the next room. *Why won't she answer?*

The kitten jumped onto Sarah's window ledge and looked into her eyes and then at the restroom door. Then back at Sarah's eyes. Then back at the door again. Sarah got up, walked over to the restroom. The kitten jumped down and darted off, back across the field.

Once inside the restroom, Sarah looked around. She saw nothing. *Was it my imagination that the cat wanted me to come in here?* Almost in tears now, just wanting to be home. *So tired.* Sarah splashed water on her face, trying not to cry. She was looking at her reflection in the mirror when she glanced down at the cups. That's where she saw it: *Jessie left a message scratched inside a cup!* She examined it closely. It read: **Window @12**. *OK! Jessie has a plan.* She filled the cup with water, drank some, dumped the rest, and wadded the cup up. She left it in the sink and went back out to her bed. Tap, tap, tap . . .

CHAPTER 43

Good Cop/Bad Mad

It was a little over an hour when the ranger knocked on Jessie's door and opened it. "Here's your supper," he said, placing the tray on the operating table. "It's not home cooking, but it is edible." He chuckled.

"What did Dr. Pubic say? Do I get to see Sarah or not?"

"They're mad, Jessie."

"Yes! That is obvious, or we wouldn't be here now! Would we?"

"Touché" the ranger laughed. "But on a serious note," he said in almost a whisper, "Jessie, my wife and two daughters were among the first experiments here. They didn't even last four months. They've come a long way in their technology, if that's what you want to call it."

"Sorry to hear about your family, but they're dead, and I am waiting to be murdered. So quite frankly, I don't give a shit. Do I get to see Sarah or not?"

"You guys really pissed them off, Jessie," he said, trying to play good cop.

"Yes or no? I will not agree to anything until I see Sarah!"

"Look, Dr. Pubic . . ." the ranger stopped, his face turning white. He looked scared. Looking at the corner between the restroom and the window, he corrected himself. "Dr. Plubblix, Plubblix is still really ticked at you two! The masters said if you girls don't cause any problems tonight—no yelling, no kicking or hitting the walls, no opening windows or anything that will cause disturbances—they will consider it. Everybody is tired, and they want no problems tonight."

The whistle sounded . . .

The ranger looked hard at the corner between the restroom and the window again. "Be good tonight, and you will most likely see Sarah in the morning." He turned and walked swiftly out.

Jessie, looking at the corner where the ranger had looked, was thinking, *That's where the camera is. I know I won't get to see Sarah in the morning. They won't let me, I'm sure. But that's OK! Twelve at the window!* There is one problem: *No clock! Damn! I'll use my instincts and Sarah will do the same. All will work! It must!*

———⁓⁓⟨⟩⁓⁓———

The ranger opened Sarah's door. Sarah jumped up to the opposite side of the bed. He walked in with her supper. Placing it on the table next to her bed, he said, "Jessie agreed to make no problems tonight, so she can see you in the morning. So she can tell you she has agreed to do the procedure, the third term. Just so they will spare you! That means no hitting or kicking the walls, no trying to get into each other's room through the restroom. No yelling or opening windows . . . no problems at all, or you will never, ever see Jessie again! Get it?"

"Bite me, Ranger!"

"No, thank you. I'm not into that. But I do know someone who is! Remember, smart-ass? Or you will never see her alive again!" He turned and left her room.

———⁓⁓⟨⟩⁓⁓———

The ranger went to Heather's room next. As he walked in with her dinner, she just lay there. He placed her dinner on the table next to her bed. "Here's your supper. Can you get up to eat it, fat ass?"

"Where is Richard? Did you kill him like you did Daniel?" Heather asked.

"How are you feeling today, Heather? I must say, you look like a beached whale." The ranger laughed.

"Get out!"

"I'm going. You remember, though! If you dare try to communicate with the other room, they will make you carry for another week. Maybe even two! Got it?" He sneered at Heather, standing by the door.

"Get out! I can't take this! Just leave!" she cried.

"I'm going! I didn't know it was possible for such a hottie like you were, could stretch this much! It's kinda fun to look at. OOOOOWie. Have a great night!" He let the door close behind him.

CHAPTER 44

Manipulation

The ranger turned to leave Heather's room, and there stood Dr. Plubblix. The ranger almost ran into him. Quickly jumping back, he sputtered, "Oh shit, you startled me."

"I have that effect on a lot of *people*. Good job, Ranger. I especially like how sincere you were when you were talking about your wife and daughters."

"That was in the beginning, Master. Damn near eight years ago. How were you to know that women can't stay pregnant for over a year? Trial and error, not your fault, Master," the ranger said, with his head bowed low.

"Do you think they are all calm for the night? I will not have any problems while I am getting ready for the big day."

"They're all good. And I'm 99 percent sure that Jessie will be more than willing in the morning. Oh yeah, Jessie wants to see and talk to Sarah before she tells you that she's ready. What do you think?" asked the ranger.

"Yes, I am quite sure *that* will happen." The doctor laughed.

"I have to get to town, talk with the bartender, and get one to replace him. It's getting late, already nine o'clock. I'll bring you your dinner. I will be back soon, Master."

"Yes, I will see you soon." Plubblix turned to leave. Then turned back quickly. "Oh, one more thing, Ranger, did you do that Dr. Pubic thing intentionally? Was it for Jessie's benefit or what?" His eyes were glowing brighter now.

"Of course, Master." The ranger bowed as he said that.

"Very well, then. You may live. Did I say 'live?'" Plubblix snickered. "What I meant was, you may leave."

The ranger bowed again, turned, and walked down the hall to the stairs.

CHAPTER 45

Pause

Jessie went over and looked at her food, then pushed it away. She was too nauseated to eat. Also, she didn't really trust eating the food. *I bet they poisoned it.* She yawned and stretched for show. Went back to her bed and sat on it for a few minutes. She got up and went to the restroom. *There it is! The cup with the message, crumpled in the sink. Sarah got the message! Unless . . . no, don't go there!* She finished in the restroom and went back to her bed. She lay there, staring up at the ceiling for a while. Then she began to toss and turn. She sat straight up, still looking at the ceiling, said, "Will you please turn off the lights so I can sleep . . . please!"

The lights went out. She lay back and did not move. She waited.

Sarah was in her room, pretending to sleep, when the lights went out. *Great!* She lay there and waited.

CHAPTER 46

New Overseer

The ranger went to Bellowing Hollers to inform the bartender of his new position and go over the duties with him. He also needed to appoint a new bartender. He walked into the bar and saw an elderly woman sitting there, drinking coffee. Featus was trailing behind him. He walked up to her and said, "Excuse me, ma'am, but today's your lucky day."

She turned deathly pale and just stared at Featus in horror.

The ranger laughed loudly. "It's not what you think!"

"W-what is it?"

"You're the new bartender!" the ranger announced and then looked intently at the now ex-bartender.

The former bartender stopped what he was doing. He froze, mouth open, and stared at the ranger.

The ranger, talking to the ex-bartender, now said, "We need to talk," and then walked to the back room, motioning for him to follow. He looked down at Featus. "Will you terrori . . . .entertain these fine folks while I talk to Jake, here?"

Featus turned and ran out the door, down the street toward the graveyard. The ranger took Jake in the back to explain his new position and go over the rules. They finished in the backroom and went back into the bar. Jake was all smiles because he knew now that he would be spared when the masters decided to end this town.

The ranger made a big production when he introduced Jake as the new overseer. Everybody in the bar cheered for Jake, thinking now they may have a chance, being that Jake was really just one of them. Jake went off with the ranger in his SUV to be detailed in and shown his new duties as the overseer.

They stopped in front of the Five & Dime to pick up Featus. The ranger turned to Jake before they walked in and told him, "I bet your first act as the new overseer will be to get a new storekeeper." They walked in and there stood Featus, finishing up with Daniel.

Jake stood there, repulsed.

"Go get the undertaker to dispose of his body. Lock the store up for the night so I can finish going over everything with you," the ranger barked out orders.

Jake turned to do what he was told to do without saying a word.

There was a lady walking swiftly by trying not to draw attention from anyone. The ranger called her over and told her, "It's OK, ma'am, I just have a quick question for you."

The lady approached hesitantly; she feared for her life.

"I was wondering, did you witness what happened here, by any chance?"

The lady shook her head frantically. She turned to walk away, keeping her head down.

"Well," the ranger walked over to her. "Let's go now, so you don't have to see this mess here." He guided her to his vehicle and helped her up inside.

Jake and the undertaker approached the store. After a few more words, the undertaker went inside, and Jake went to the SUV and got in. The ranger, Featus, Jake, and the lady drove off past the graveyard. The ranger filled Jake in on the way to Dr. Plubblix's house. The lady just sat there, afraid to open her mouth. "And don't forget Jake, don't ever, ever say or even think anything but sweet thoughts about Featus or anyone he cares about. Got it?"

"Yes, sir, I got it" Jake answered as he helped the lady out of the SUV.

"Come on, ma'am, you need to see the doctor—no, what I meant is, the doctor needs you!" the ranger said, then began to laugh hysterically. He guided her into the house, with Jake and Featus tagging along behind him. The ranger delivered the lady to Plubblix.

He showed Jake around the house and explained the house duties thoroughly. Featus was walking along behind them. "Now come, it's near midnight. We must get you back to town so I can do what I do."

CHAPTER 47

Action Point

Jessie was dozing off, when suddenly she heard a thud on her window. It was her *lifesaver!* She didn't want to draw attention to her room, so she didn't sit right up. She arranged her pillow and the sheets to make it appear she was lying there. She slid out from under the covers and, staying in the shadows, crawled to the window. She stood there, staring out. *If they suspect anything, they'll react soon.* She stood there, not moving for at least five minutes. No lights were turned on. OK, *everything is fine.* So far . . .

———⚬⚬⚬⚬⚬⚬⚬———

Sarah was lying in bed, looking out of the window, when she saw the kitten jump up on the window ledge and then back down. She too arranged her bed to make it look as though she was lying there. She walked in the shadows to the window and stood there waiting, looking at the kitten.

———⚬⚬⚬⚬⚬⚬⚬———

The kitten sat in the middle of the windows, about five feet away on a tree limb. There were no clouds this night. The moon was bright, three-quarters full. Perfect for what was about to happen.

Sarah stared at the kitten. The kitten was staring at her and then looked to Jessie, who was at the other window. Then looked back to

Sarah. Sarah reached to open the window. "*No! Don't open the window. I will relay the conversation.*" Sarah asked, *What?* in her mind. "*It's me, Frawas, that is my name. Sarah, Jessie, let's plan. If someone walks in, disconnect eye contact. If it is the little one, think black over and over until you see black in your head. Like you did earlier, Jessie. You see, he can read your thoughts without me being present. The others you need not worry about, unless I'm at hand. And if I'm there, simply think black. Got it?*"

Yes, both of the girls thought.

"*Let's get on with the plan, now. J.R. and his friend will come tomorrow night. The friend will break in and help you escape. The friend is weird. I can relay to J.R. what's happening, but not to her. I can't receive any of her images, she can't receive mine either. She's different, but that's perfect, you see. They won't be able to detect her coming at all. We think. They most likely won't be able to sense J.R, we hope. Anyway, J.R. will sneak into town.*" The thought process started happening so fast. Sarah thought she wouldn't be able to keep up. Jessie just absorbed it all. Frawas was going over all tomorrow night's details as quickly as she could and hoped the girls would understand.

"*What do we do?*" asked Jessie.

"*Wait where you are.*"

The lights suddenly came on. Frawas took off. The girls just stood there, staring out the window.

The intercom broke through the silence, "What is going on in there?"

"Why are you asking me a question that must be answered, if you can't hear me?" Jessie answered.

"I can't sleep. I'm thinking about Jessie. How is she doing? I want to see her. Please" Sarah said, looking up at the corner where she believed the camera was.

The voice said in Sarah's room, "We will see what we can do for you, Sarah. But for now, you must sleep. It will be a big day for all!"

Oh shit. Then Sarah yelled, "What's happening tomorrow?"

Jessie, still looking out the window, yelled, "I know you can hear us!" She could not see the kitten anywhere. She went to the restroom door, it clicked, and she went inside again. She stayed in there for a few minutes. She exited and went to lie down. The lights went out again.

Sarah and Jessie slept.

CHAPTER 48

I've Got to Go

Jessie woke up early the next morning. She jumped right out of bed and ran to the restroom door, tried it. It did not open. "I have to pee!" she bellowed, looking up into the corner, dancing around.

The voice over the intercom, "The restroom must be cleaned before you enter."

"You don't understand, I really have to pee, man."

"You must wait. Jake will be in, in about an hour or so to clean up in there."

"OK, I'll pee in that sink, then, because I really need to go! Really, really bad!" Jessie said, as she walked over to the sink.

"Make it quick." The restroom door clicked to unlock it.

She ran back over to the door and entered. She really did have to go. She finished, washed her hands, and looked at the cups. There was nothing scratched in them. She started to go out. Then hesitated. She went back to the stack and separated them. There it was, etched in the middle cup. It read: *Agree2nothin!* She filled the cup with water and moved out of the restroom.

———❦———

Sarah had awakened and walked to the restroom door. She tried it. It was locked. "Open the door, I've got to go!" She tried the door again. It would not open. "Open the door! I really have to go!" It still would not release.

The intercom voice reverberated, "You must wait! Jake will be in to check and clean the restroom."

Sarah paced the room.

—————⁓⁓⚬⚬⊙⊙⚬⊙⊙⊙⚬⊙⊙⚬⚬⁓⁓—————

Jake opened Jessie's door then knocked as an afterthought. Jessie was staring out the window, with a cup of water in her hand. "I see they recruited another flunkie. How long do you think you will last?"

"Good morning to you, Jessie. Here's your breakfast." Jake placed it on the operating table and then moved toward the restroom where Jessie was standing. Jessie moved to the operating table. He looked up at the corner, the door clicked unlocked. He opened the door and walked inside. The door closed behind him.

Jessie stood on the other side of the operating table and waited for Jake to come out. She heard the rattle of the main door. It did not open. Five minutes later, Jake walked out. "I need my bag so I can shower!"

"I'll see what I can do."

"Yeah, right! I'm going to shower now, with or without it. Hey man, where is the ranger? Did they slay him too?"

"No, he's not dead. He's doing what he does."

"Oh, I see. Playing preacher, trying to trap some other poor souls."

"What?" Jake looked puzzled at Jessie for a couple of seconds.

The doorknob rattled again. Jake walked over to it and opened it. Featus ran in.

Immediately, Jessie started thinking, *Black, black, black . . .* until all she saw in her mind was black. Featus approached Jessie. She finished her water and crumpled the cup. *Black, black, black . . .* Featus walked right up to her and stared into her eyes. *Black, black, black . . .* While thinking this, she also began to think, *"I won't do what they ask!" They're going to kill Sarah! KILL SARAH! Black, black, black . . .* Featus bared his teeth. Jessie was yelling out in her brain, if that's possible. *They want to kill Sarah! KILL SARAH! Black, black, black . . .* Was that a growl? *Black . . .*

Featus turned abruptly and sprinted toward the door, ramming into Jake on the way out. Jake stumbled but caught himself before he fell. "What did you do?"

Jessie smirked at Jake and walked to the restroom. "I want to shower now," she said, looking up into the corner between the window and restroom. Then *click*, she opened the door and went inside.

Sarah was pacing around the room. "I really have got to go!" she hollered.

The voice over the speaker said, "Jessie is in the shower. You must wait."

Sarah walked over to the restroom door and kicked it. "I have to pee, Jessie! Hurry up!"

Jessie heard that. She hurried and put her same clothes back on. She kicked the door that went into Sarah's room, "I'm finished!" She went to her door and exited.

Sarah went into the restroom. She looked through the cups to see if there was anything written on them. There was not. She finished her business and then decided to take a shower as well. She finished with that and put her same clothes on. She left the restroom. Jake was cleaning her room and had her breakfast sitting on her table by the bed.

"You may as well take that shit! I won't eat it, it's probably poisonous or something," Sarah said with a fake smile on her face.

Jake picked up a piece of toast and stuck it in his mouth. He chewed and swallowed it. His face turned red, eyes bulging, then he grabbed his throat and began coughing.

Sarah stood there, watching for a few seconds, and then asked, "So if you're not the bartender anymore, who took your place? And how long do you think you'll live doing this job?"

Jake stopped coughing, swallowed his toast, then answered, "I hope to have this job longer than the town will last, and yes, they do have a lady that took my place as the bartender. Thank you for your concern. By the way, my name is Jake."

"Well, I must admit it hasn't been a pleasure meeting you, or being in this so-called town."

The doorknob on the door that led to the hall rattled a little. Nobody came in. Sarah and Jake looked at it, then at one another.

Jake turned around and exited without saying another word. Sarah went to the window and stared out.

CHAPTER 49

Meeting Heather

Jessie was looking out the window, trying to find some sign of Frawas. Straining her eyes to see in the shadows of the trees. Just then her bedroom door opened. Jessie spun around quickly, "Well, well, if it isn't Dr. Freakystein! Do I get to see Sarah, or what?"

"J-Jessie, uh, the r-ranger s-said you will be ready to go under-g-go the um, process." His hands were shaking.

"*No!* I am not willing and never will be! I want to see Sarah!"

Plubblix, glaring at Jessie, eyes turning scarlet, now snapped, "You will not ever see Sarah until you have agreed to do the procedure!"

"I guess I won't see her then. I never came to this godforsaken town of my own free will, nor will I ever agree to do a damn thing for you or anybody in this place! You guys are a bunch of sick and twisted—"

"We really do not need you, you selfish little bitch. Sarah has decided to go ahead with it." Plubblix said, walking toward her, his eyes brighter than ever now. His hands no longer shaking, and his demeanor arrogant, he continued, "Sarah did not want to see you hurt, so she has agreed!"

Jessie held her ground and went nose to nose with Plubblix, "You are a liar! You and all your little cohorts are nothing—a bunch of nobodies. You guys manipulate and murder, without thinking twice."

Now his eyes were bloody crimson, looking like flames burning. He stated, "I think I will have you witness the procedure to your

144

so-called friend! I will give you a front-row seat! And only then can little Master Featus finish you!"

"Screw you! You, Dr. Pube, are nothing but a pretender! Sarah has agreed to nothing! She never will either, so you might as well murder us now!" She was so mad, she lunged at him and hit him in the chest. He had to take a step backward to maintain his balance.

"Why, you little—"

"Get the hell out of here, you freak!"

"No, you are going to listen to me, Jessie!" He was walking toward her, his eyes still shimmering. Jessie took a step back. Plubblix hurdled at her so quickly she didn't even see him coming. He grabbed both of her arms and twisted them in front until she could not move. "Oh, you will concur. That is the fact of the matter!" He was pulling her to the door. "The third term is not near as bad as the first or second, it is not really even an implant." He twisted one of her arms behind her as he let go of the other. He opened the door with his free hand. "I believe it will not be a strain on your physical being. I will not have you or Sarah determine the fate of my species!" He was walking her past Sarah's room to Heather's room. "I have it down now and understand the human body completely. I know how much a woman can bear!" He stopped in front of Heather's door. "This woman is at her limit. One of you *will* consent to do the third and most likely final term!" He twisted the doorknob. "I am superior to earth's doctors. I may be able to spare either you or Sarah, depending on who is willing to go on with this first. And most likely both of you will live, if you authorize me to go ahead on you."

Plubblix pushed the door open and shoved Jessie inside. She stopped, mortified, staring at Heather. Jessie cried out, "What have you done!" *Bick's daughter.* The girl just lay there. Heather was huge! She was unable to move or even turn her head. There were tubes and wires running in and out of her body. Tears came to Jessie's eyes. "What have you done?" This time her voice was coming out as a whimper.

The doctor said to Heather, sounding cheerful, "G-good, uh-morning, H-Heather."

"Good morning, Doctor," Heather whispered, sounding like she was in pain.

"How are you f-feeling this wonderful, um, m-morning?"

"It's really getting bad, I feel like I'm going to pop."

"It will all be over soon," the doctor told Heather.

Jessie cried out, "Are you going to kill her?"

"No," the doctor said, calmly. "That's where you c-come in. I b-believe, um, if we do this operation today, or uh in the morning at the latest, Heather may be able to, uh, be spared. This is, you see, why, I uh, we need your co-oper . . . co . . . uh, approval as quickly as p-possible. W-we must p-prep you. You see?"

Jessie turned away from Heather. Wiping her tears, she walked to the door.

The doctor turned to Heather, "My d-dear, I will, uh, be back after I take J-Jessie here to her r-room. Um, OK?"

"Yes, doctor."

The doctor opened the door and guided Jessie out. He had no reason to restrain her. She was tranquil after what she had just observed. They walked slowly down the hall to Jessie's door. The doctor opened the door and held it for Jessie. Jessie entered and immediately spotted Frawas sleeping on the window ledge. She stopped abruptly. The doctor ran into the back of her. She turned around and drastically started to plead with him.

"I really want to help Heather! But you must let me see Sarah first. I must talk to her. Did you say for sure that Heather would live? Please let me see and talk with Sarah."

"I am n-ninety-eight, um, percent sure that Heather will indeed live. She will be just like, uh, new once we extract the l-little one."

"There is no way she will ever be just like new! But at least she'll be alive." Jessie turned back around and walked inside. The kitten was gone.

"Oh yes, you see, uh, w-women are like elastic, they s-stretch, and with a l-little, um, cream and ex-ecer, um, with a l-little working out, she'll be just like new."

"Where did you get your information, Doctor? Women are not elastic! She's way, way too big! Her skin won't just shrink up!

Whatever, anyway, I'll need to convince Sarah that I will be fine and that she will need to cooperate with you guys."

"So you are, uh, agreeing to do the p-procedure, Jessie?"

"No! I am not agreeing to anything. Only after I make sure Sarah will be OK, then I will consent. But I think we've got to do it tomorrow morning, for fear that Heather may not last much longer."

"I see," the doctor said, squinting his eyes at Jessie. *Red eyes glowing.*

"I have one more question for you, doctor. May I?"

"Uh, s-sure." *Back to normal.*

"What are you going to do with Sarah?"

"After we do the, um, p-procedure with you and everything is f-fine for a couple of, uh, days, you see, um, S-Sarah can do whatever she wishes. Uh, you see?"

"You mean, she can visit me too?"

"Uh, s-sure."

"I really want to help that girl Heather. She won't live for much longer, you know. But . . . I need to talk with Sarah before. She's my best friend, and we always talk about everything."

"Um . . . we will s-see." The doctor turned and walked out of the room.

CHAPTER 50

Dragging

Jessie went to the window. Frawas was sitting in the same spot she had been sitting the last time she transmitted the images. The imagery began. Instantaneously, Sarah spotted the ranger walking at the other end of the field, and he was carrying a rifle, leaning against his shoulder. Frawas scrambled up to the window and slinked to the other end of the house. Jessie stood there, staring at him. Sarah went to her bed and knocked on the wall, trying to get Heather's attention. She heard moaning.

———⁓⁓o⁓⁓⁓———

After a few minutes, Jessie opened the window and yelled out, "Hey, Ranger, I tot I thaw a wabbit go da uddr way!" She slammed the window and stood there, laughing. The ranger flipped her off and walked on.

———⁓⁓o⁓⁓⁓———

Sarah continued knocking on the wall, trying to get the girl to answer her. The only thing Sarah heard were cries of agonizing pain.

———⁓⁓o⁓⁓⁓———

The hours were dragging by. Jessie was pacing around the room, stopping at the window every once in a while. The ranger was out of sight by the second stop. The kitten had not reappeared. Still pacing, Jessie heard the doorknob rattle. She froze behind the operating table. Nobody opened the door. She thought of Featus staring up in her face and then turning and ramming the bartender on his way out. This thought brought a smirk to her face. She looked up to the corner where she thought the camera was and smiled. She began to march around the room again.

Sarah, still listening to the cries from the next room, began to walk around the space. She felt like a caged animal. Suddenly she heard a knock on the door.

CHAPTER 51

The Plan

Knock . . .

"Why start with the consideration now?" Sarah shouted.

The ranger opened the door and held it for Dr. Plubblix. Following the doctor was Featus. Featus ran around the doctor and stopped directly in front of Sarah. Looking up at her, Featus said in a soft voice, "Sarah."

"Every time I see him, he appears to have gotten taller." Suddenly, she realized she needs to be thinking, *Black, black black . . . I want to see Jessie.*

"Well, uh, you s-see, um . . ."

Sarah interrupted again. "Who are you guys killing in the next room?" *Black, black, black, I want to see my best friend! Black, black, black.*

Featus, still smiling, reached his hand out to Sarah.

The doctor began again, "I, um, am trying to, uh . . ."

Sarah demanded, "Who are you killing in the next room?" *Black, black, black. I will die if I don't see Jessie! Black, black, black.*

Featus reached out and took her hand, and then said in a gentle voice, "Sarah . . . come."

Sarah pulled her hand back away from Featus and asked, "Is it Jessie? Are they killing Jessie?" *Black, black, black. Please help me, Featus. Black, black, black. I miss my best friend. Black, black, black. Please help me see her. Black, black, black.*

Featus, staring down at the floor, looked up at the top of his eyes, and then looked down again. He reached his hand up to Sarah's and said, "No, Sarah. Come."

Black, black, black.

The doctor said, "If you would j-just, uh, let me—" He stopped in mid-sentence. Featus turned, eyes glowing red, and stared at him. The doctor looked at the ranger and snapped. "Go to Heather and see if you can ease her pain some!"

Black, black, black . . .

"Yes doctor," the ranger exited.

Black, black, black . . .

"Sarah," Featus said, in an endearing voice. He took her hand and led her to the door. The doctor stepped back and opened the door for them. Featus led Sarah down the hall to Jessie's room and waited by the door. The doctor followed, fumbling for his keys to unlock the door.

Black, black, black . . .

Jessie was still striding around the room when the door opened. In walked Sarah and Featus, hand in hand, as the doctor held the door open for them. Jessie had stopped next to the operating table, "What the . . . ?"

Sarah mouthed the word *black* to Jessie. *Black, black, black . . .*

Jessie immediately began thinking, *Black, black, black . . .* Jessie turned to the doctor and asked, "Did you tell her?" *Black, black, black . . .*

"Uh, n-no."

"Well, I need to talk to Sarah, then. Privately!" Jessie snapped at the doctor. *Black, black, black . . .*

"W-well, um . . ." the doctor started.

Featus let go of Sarah's hand and turned and walked toward the door. The doctor held the door open for Featus with one arm, waiting just outside the door. Featus reached the door. Featus opened it a little wider, then the doctor stepped back into the hall and smiled at him. Featus slammed the door. The doctor stood there with a look of disbelief on his face. Featus turned around to face the girls and smiled broadly.

Sarah and Jessie looked at each other in shock. They looked at Featus and began to guffaw.

"*Black,*" Jessie laughed, looking at Sarah.

"*Yeah, black.*" Sarah cackled back.

Featus just stood there, smiling at them.

Black, black, black . . . both of the girls were thinking. They knew they had to plan their escape, but how with Featus in the room with them? *Black, black, black.*

"I'm hungry, Sarah. *Black, black, black* . . ."

Black, black, black . . . *Featus, I'm hungry too.* "So am I." *Black, black, black* . . .

Featus went to the door, knocked once, and looked at the corner where the camera was presumed to be. The door opened and there stood the ranger. Featus looked up at him, said nothing, and then slammed the door in his face. He turned back around to face the girls and smiled once again.

Jessie, laughing, asked Sarah, "What was that about?" *Black, black, black* . . .

"Featus told him to bring us some food." *Black, black, black* . . .

"OK. Can he talk regular, though?" Jessie questioned. *Black, black, black* . . .

Sarah looked at Featus. *Black, black, black* . . . Then back at Jessie. "Somewhat, but why should he when he gets his point across?"

Black, black, black . . . "Right on."

"I'm glad we get to see each other," Sarah said to Jessie. *Black, black, black* . . .

"Yeah, man, me too." *Black, black, black* . . . "They want me to do the procedure first thing in the morning," Jessie told Sarah in a stage-like voice. *Black, black, black* . . .

"That's the rumor. What are you going to do?" *Black, black, black* . . .

Black, black, black . . . In that bad acting voice, Jessie said, "Well, the girl in the room next to you is named Heather. Did you know that?" *Black, black, black* . . .

The train whistle began to sound, nonstop.

Sarah looked at Featus. Featus went to the door, looked at the camera in the corner, and the door clicked. He opened it and walked out. The door closed behind him.

Sarah and Jessie hugged each other. The whistle continued its nonstop scream. Jessie, talking in almost a yell over the high-pitched screech, said, "We need to try to hang with each other tonight. I have a good feeling about tonight! We're leaving this hellhole! Can you control Featus?"

"I don't know, I just ask him in my mind, and he does stuff."

"Let's try to stay together tonight so it will be easier for the escape."

The whistle shriek stopped.

The girls continued holding one another, both acting afraid. The door opened, and in walked the ex-bartender, Jake. Holding the door open he said, "The ranger will be back shortly with your food." He turned to depart, Featus ran in. Jake flinched as Featus ran past him. He exited, the door closed behind him.

Black, black black . . . "Think black!" whispered Sarah. *Black, black, black* . . . Sarah looked at Featus. He walked toward her with a wide smile on his face. Sarah turned back to Jessie, who was now sitting on the bed, and said, "Featus had them turn off that scary noise." *Black, black, black* . . .

Jessie turned to Featus, "Thank you, Featus. It was scary! How is it you seem to grow every time I see you?" *Black, black, black* . . .

Featus squinted at Jessie, looking at her out of the corner of his red, glowing eyes.

Sarah quickly continued the conversation they were having before the whistle sounded. "I didn't know her name was Heather." *Black, black, black* . . . "I've heard her crying and carrying on all morning. I thought they were killing you or something. What's wrong with her?" *Black, black, black* . . .

Black, black, black . . . "Oh, Sarah, you would cry too if you saw her. I think it's Bick's daughter. She is about ready to pop!"

The whistle started again.

Featus looked at the corner where the camera was hidden and bared his teeth. His eyes were glowing brighter than before.

The shriek squeal of the whistle stopped immediately.

Featus looked at Sarah and grinned.

Black, black, black . . . "Now, Featus is getting real pissed because they keep interrupting." *Black, black, black . . .*

"OK then." *Black, black, black . . .* "The doctor introduced me to Heather. He thinks if I hurry and agree to do the third term, he can spare her life. Also, the third term may be the final one." *Black, black, black . . .*

"Do you know exactly what is going on, Jessie?" *Black, black, black . . .*

At that moment, the ranger walked in with two bags of food. He placed them on the operating table and said, "Pastrami sandwiches."

"Thanks," the girls said together.

Featus, looking at the ranger through his little red slits that were his eyes, began to walk slowly toward him. The ranger started swiftly out of the room.

Sarah and Jessie opened their bags and began to eat. Sarah offered Featus half of hers. He declined.

"I didn't realize I was this hungry," Jessie stated.

Black, black, black . . . "I know, and this food isn't bad either."

"Yep!" Jessie agreed as she took another bite. *Black, black, black . . .* The sun was beginning to set as they ate. "I feel I must help that black poor girl. So in the morning I will agree. But I want to spend time with you tonight!" *Black, black, black . . .*

"But what exactly, is going to happen? Do you know?"

Black, black, black . . . "All I know is that it is not an implant. I will be hooked up to tubes with that black creature."

Featus looked angrily at Jessie for a few seconds.

"I mean, with the baby," Jessie corrected. *Black, black, black . . .*

"This is weird and black!" Sarah commanded. *Black, black, black . . .*

Black, black, black . . . "Yeah, and I don't want to talk about it anymore, man!" Jessie added.

They began to talk about the past when they were in high school. They tried to have Featus join in their chat. They were sitting on the bed now, facing each other. Featus was standing next to the bed, watching Sarah. In their conversation every once in a while they would throw in the word black just as a reminder.

Jessie got up to stretch. She was facing the window. It was dark outside now. Featus walked over and stood next to Jessie. She continued to stand there, staring out the window, having an exchange with Sarah. Jessie thought she saw some little red speck out in the field. *Black, black, black . . . just like the night Steve was killed and in the night terrors! Black, black, black . . . they're heading toward the house. Black, black, black . . . Black, black, black . . .* She began to think it harder. *Black, black, black.*

Featus looked up at Jessie's face and glared into her eyes, as if trying to read something. He stared for a couple of minutes.

Black, black, black . . . Black, black, black . . . Only concentrating on her "black" thought. *Black, black, black . . .*

Featus's eyes were slits of glittering crimson. He appeared to be transforming into something evil. Reading, reading what? He broke the gaze and looked back at Sarah. His eyes just slightly red, and his face almost back to normal. In an endearing voice, he said, "Sarah."

Sarah, confused at the total change with Jessie and Featus, looked back and forth between them. *Black, black, black . . .*

Jessie looked at her and shook her head. *Black, black, black . . .*

Sarah nodded as if to say she understood what Jessie was trying to say.

When suddenly, Frawas jumped on the window's ledge, puffed up, hissed.

CHAPTER 52

The Escape

Featus turned to the window where Frawas was and hissed. His eyes were, in fact, bloodred and his face transforming into that evil being once again. A split-second later, he was hitting the bars on the outside of the window with his head. And then they heard the glass shattering. His head bent the bars outward. Featus lay on the floor, his head split open and blood pouring from the wound. He was out.

They heard a loud meow.

The whistle began to sound violently.

Sarah and Jessie darted over to the window. There sat Frawas, curled up on the edge of the roof, staring at the two girls. The thought images started immediately after Sarah looked into the kitten's eyes.

The dream that Sarah had flashed into their minds. The car hitting the mailbox and the mail flying everywhere. The ranger running across the street as the mail flew. J.R. was driving. He spun a brody, then punched it as the ranger approached. A fight between two boys they went to high school with. Jessie's mother riding a motorcycle. The ranger running back to his truck and taking off after J.R.

Sarah broke the connection and the images stopped. Sarah bawled to Jessie, "What's all this mean?" There was the squeal of the whistle still going off.

The door burst open, in ran the ranger and the doctor.

Jessie and Sarah leaned over Featus, trying to look as though they were helping him.

The doctor shoved Jessie out of the way. He stopped abruptly; looking up into space for a few seconds, grabbed the ranger's arm, and demanded, "Get to town! There is something about to happen!"

At that moment, Frawas jumped up on the window ledge again, and she stared at the doctor, who was now bending over Featus, trying to examine him. The doctor looked into Frawas's eyes, and the images began to fly. This went on for what seemed like a few minutes, until Frawas broke the connection and ran. She dove off the roof and hit the ground. She was trying to find a way inside to Jessie and Sarah.

After Frawas took off, the doctor quickly looked about the room for the girls. They were gone. *They must have followed the ranger out.* The doctor stood up to go search for them, then stopped and bent down to pick up Featus—he couldn't just leave him. The doctor carried Featus with him to search for the girls. With the brief examination, he could tell that Featus was already beginning to heal. Where his head was split open was no longer bleeding and was actually closing up. *No stitches required.* The doctor laughed to himself. He was racing down the hallway when he heard Heather's ear-piercing shriek over the sound of the whistle. *Hold on just a little while longer, my dear, your pain will soon be over.*

Sarah and Jessie did follow the ranger out. Jessie caught the door just before it closed. Sarah was on her tail. They ran the opposite way of Heather's room. They too heard Heather crying out, but there was nothing they could do to help her right now. They knew they had to help themselves first. Jessie bypassed a door on her right. Sarah tried the door, "It's stairs!" Jessie turned back around and followed Sarah down the flight of steps. When they reached the bottom, the door was locked. "Shit!" Sarah said, after trying the door.

"Damn it!" Jessie said as she turned to run back upstairs, taking two at a time. When she reached the top, that door was locked as well. They were trapped in the stairwell. They turned and ran back down the steps. "Let's kick it by the doorknob together, maybe it'll give." They did so, and the door didn't budge. They stopped, leaning against the wall, Sarah, out of breath asked, "Did you get anything out of the images from Frawas?"

Jessie said, "I'm not sure, man. It was like everything we've already experienced. Don't you think?"

"Yeah, we have to try this again. On the count of three, ready?"

"No, it hurt my foot!"

"We're stuck here, man! We have to try something!"

They heard the clatter of somebody messing with the door lock. "Oh shit!" Sarah whispered and turned to run back up the stairs. Jessie was on her tail. After they reached the top, Sarah whispered, "Now what?"

"I don't know, man. Let's hide up here, and when he comes around the corner, we'll push him down the stairs and take his keys to get out. If he gets me, you keep going! No matter what! Promise me?"

"OK, I promise, but you have to do the same! Promise?" begged Sarah.

"All right!"

They waited there, quietly, listening. They heard the door squeak open. The door closed but did not lock. They heard the sound of shoes tip-tapping up the stairwell. Sarah squeezed Jessie's arm tightly as they were ready to fight. Finally the person rounded the corner, Jessie's arms up, ready to shove, when she noticed who it was.

"Mom!" Jessie squealed with astonishment.

At the same time, Sarah burst out, "Joan?"

CHAPTER 53

The Blowout

"*Mom*, what are you doing here?"

"SHhhh . . ." She took Jessie and Sarah's hands and gave them a quick squeeze. "Come on, we must hurry!" She let go of Sarah's hand and started down the stairs, still holding Jessie's. The girls followed closely. They reached the bottom and stopped. Joan turned around, facing the girls, and said, "You must try to have a clear mind. It's working as planned so far, but we have got to hurry. I have a motorcycle out at the edge of the grass over that way." She pointed in the direction where the bike was waiting. "The only way out is to follow the tree line through the graveyard to the road, and then don't look back, just keep on it! Jessie, I know you can ride. Sarah, you hold on to her and lean into the turns! The bike is ready to start, just kick it! It is facing the direction you must go. Go just past the church and then stop in the turnout on the right-hand side. I have my ride put out of sight in the trees. Wait for me for no longer than five hours! If I'm not there by then—leave! You will be safe until then. There will be one more g—" The door at the top of the stairway opened. "You girls go—now! I will distract them! Go!" Joan pushed the girls to get them running.

She closed the door, picked up her baseball bat. The door opened, out ran the doctor. He spotted the girls running through the field and started after them. Joan ran up behind him and hit him in the back as hard as she could, and then she took off toward the town.

———❦———

Joan ran through the trees until she reached Bellowing Hollers. It was total chaos. *Just as planned!* People were running throughout the street. Joan could see her ride at the other end of town. She took off at a dead run toward the graveyard and toward the vehicle waiting for her. The ranger was just reaching his SUV as she ran past. His vehicle roared to life and flung gravel at her as he flew past, after the car that had just finished ramming the mailbox and starting all this madness. Joan was running as fast as she could, but it was no use. The car had to go! That was what the plan was, go with or without her. Not under any circumstances was he to be caught. The main priority is to help the girls escape. He had to go! He punched it and was on his way. The ranger was on his tail. They were barreling down the road, passing the cemetery.

———❦———

Jessie got to the road when she noticed the two automobiles rushing toward them. She gave it all it had— opened the throttle up fully. They left the other two vehicles quite a distance behind them.

———❦———

The ranger was gaining on him, when suddenly there was a loud boom, and his vehicle began to weave back and forth as it slowed.

Thank God it was a blowout! Joan thought as she watched the chase then heard the explosion. She took off, sprinting back behind the graveyard, trying to make her way to meet the trio. She had to move it if she was going to meet them. It was over twenty miles away.

———❦———

Jessie and Sarah passed the church, and began to slow, looking to the right for the turnout. They reached the destination within fifteen minutes of the time they left the edge of the meadow. They looked for Joan's automobile and found it buried behind some bushes. They pushed the bike behind the shrubs as well. She started her mother's VW bus. It was good to go. Everything worked, it fired right up, a full tank of gas, the lights worked!

"We're ready to rock and roll as soon as mom gets here."

"How did she know, Jessie?"

"Man, I think she knew before anybody knew. Wait . . . do you hear that? It sounds like a car."

"Yeah, I hear it. Oh, Jessie, I'm scared. What if it's not your mom?"

"Don't sweat it, it will be."

The vehicle slowed as it approached. The headlights shined through the bushes; they went off. Somebody got out of the car and started walking toward the bus. Jessie grabbed a tire iron. Sarah locked her door and started checking to make sure the rest were locked. She went to search for some sort of weapon in the back. As the person neared, Jessie turned the headlight high beams on. "Oh, man," Jessie said before she jumped out.

"Don't go . . ." Sarah started to say, when she noticed who it was.

She jumped out and ran over to them. "J.R., we thought you were long gone! How did you know?"

Jessie cut in, "Did you and my mom plan this?"

"Yeah, but . . ." he mumbled.

"But what, J.R? Did something happen to her?"

"Not that I . . . know-bah, I had to . . . go-bah."

"You left her there? Let's go get her, man!" She started walking to the car.

"Bah-you can't, she said to . . . wait-bah, or you may be . . . bait-bah."

Jessie got to the door of the car J.R. had driven up in. "I will not leave my mother to be tortured by those freaks!"

"There's no . . . fuel-bah. That's why we can't . . . duel-bah."

"We're out of gas? Let's take the bus then!"

"Your mom said . . . wait-bah, and in four and a half hours . . . not to hesitate-bah! We must . . . cower-bah. We have to . . . leave-bah, even if it's not what we . . . believe-bah!"

"I can't just sit here!"

"Jessie," Sarah said, "your mother did say to wait. Remember? And then we are to leave if she doesn't make it on time. We will get help, a *lot* of help, and get her out then."

"I can't just sit here!"

"We have to trust what she said. She'll be here soon, it's just going to take a little longer if she's on foot."

"It will take a lot longer! She saved us! I can't just leave her!"

"There will be no . . . vote-bah, but I do have . . . a note-bah." J.R. walked over to the bus and retrieved the note from the glovebox and handed it to Jessie.

Sarah and Jessie followed. He handed the note to Jessie, got inside the bus and stretched out in the backseat. Sarah got in the front and locked the doors again. Jessie went to the driver's side and hit the lights off and just held the note. She was trying not to cry.

After a few minutes, Jessie composed herself. She read:

Jessie —

I know this is all very weird. We can laugh about it later. I've always wanted more adventure in my life. Well, I really got what I asked for this time! I never wanted to hurt you or your sister with my abnormalities. I am who I am. I can't do better than that. If I don't make it back on time, you have to leave! Things get very weird around 2 a.m. I know you'll want to go after me to save me — please don't! Just go get help! You must! Nobody knows I am up here because, as you well know, NOBODY ever believes a word I say. That's par for the course. Oh well, I escaped from the ward because I had a strange feeling about what was going on with you two girls. I'm thankful I met up with J.R. He's a little strange, but he is dedicated! Go with him to get help, he will see this through. Please listen to me on this one.

I love you very much!
MOM

CHAPTER 54

Frawas

The three of them sat in the bus and waited for Joan to arrive. They weren't talking much. Time was dragging by, but when it was time to leave it seemed that they had just begun to wait. It was near 2:00 a.m., and they had to go. Jessie and Sarah were in tears. Jessie was driving, Sarah in the passenger seat. J.R. was in the back, lying on the seat. She started the VW. "At least we'll leave the bike for her, so she'll have some way of escape when she gets here. J.R., why don't you move that car in where we were to get it out of sight."

"Without a . . . doubt-bah. Just let me . . . out-bah."

Jessie stopped the bus, and J.R. got out and moved it to where the bus had been parked. He checked to make sure the keys were in the bike ignition; they were. Sarah had gotten out and started putting some brush in front of the car. J.R. helped her. Jessie turned the bus around and put her headlights on them. The car was completely covered. She hollered for them, "Come guys, you can't see it. We've got to go! I am getting a really freaky feeling, man!" They ran to the bus and got in. "Do you guys see that?" She pointed out in the direction from where they had come.

"Oh shit! Let's get the hell out of here!" Sarah demanded.

"She's . . . right, Jessie-bah. I have no . . . fight-bah, and this could get . . . messy-bah!"

Jessie put it in first gear and began to roll forward, when she noticed that the red specks were getting closer. "They're coming for us, man!"

"It's not like before, Jessie. There's only one set. Remember the last time we saw something like this, there were hundreds, maybe even thousands."

"I don't care, Sarah! I'm out of here!" Jessie continued rolling slow due to the potholes. The red specks were closing in on them. They were almost at the street when the VW died. The bus's lights were still on, but it would not fire up. "I think I know what it is! Mom's bus always has this problem. J.R., grab the tire iron and guard while I fix it. I hope it's what I think!"

J.R. slid the sliding door open. Sarah got out too, "I'm not staying in there by myself!"

"Well, grab a weapon of some sort! That demon wannabe is getting closer! I have an eerie feeling!" Jessie said.

Sarah picked up a screwdriver and ran to the back where J.R. was waiting. Jessie had the flashlight she retrieved from under the seat that was directly behind the driver's seat. She turned it on—nothing! She shook it, pointed it at the engine, and turned it on. It came on for a couple of seconds, then it went out.

"Shit! It is that wire, it came off the coil!" She unscrewed the flashlight and took both the batteries out. She rubbed the ends together, and as she was putting them back in, she dropped one. "Shit! I dropped it, help me find it." It was so dark she could not see where it fell. The fog was rolling in from the direction of Bellowing Hollers. Sarah and J.R. were searching blindly with their hands, trying to find the batteries. There was a spark! It made Sarah scream. "What in the . . ." Jessie had started to say, and then realized what it was.

"I have a . . . lighter-bah, to make it . . . brighter-bah."

"Here's the battery, Jessie!" Sarah said excitedly.

Jessie looked at Sarah and smirked at her, "Hold the lighter right here so I can put the wire back in place." Jessie took the wire and touched it to the coil. "Ouch! It shocked me! Shit. Hold on, I forgot to turn the key off." She ran to the driver's side, reached in and turned the key off.

"Hurry, my thumb is . . . burning-bah, and it's very . . . concerning-bah."

Jessie raced around to the back end of the bus. "Let it go for a few! You don't have to stand there and hold it on!" she snapped. While kneeling down, she reached inside the engine compartment, fumbling for the wire, "You can light it now!"

J.R. relit the lighter for her, "You forgot your . . . medication-bah. You need to get some . . . dedication-bah."

Jessie looked sharply at J.R., then back to her business of putting the wire back where it belonged. "Let's go!" She stood and looked through the back window. She grabbed J.R. and Sarah's arm. "Look inside." There it was, a glowing animal's eye, shining, perched up on the dashboard. "Let's get it! There are three of us, and only one of it!"

J.R. broke loose and ran to the passenger side. He opened the door—the crimson specks darted into J.R.'s chest. "Bah!"

Sarah screamed as she and Jessie ran over to help J.R.

"Bah-ha-ha, bah-ha-ha. Frawas . . . bah has sharp . . . claws-bah! Bah-ha-ha."

The girls both ran to pet the lifesaving kitten. The fog was still preceding their way. Jessie ran around the front of the bus and got in. The bus started right up. Looking hard in the direction from where the kitten had come, she did not see her mother. "Well, it's after two now. We've got to head out, man." She began progressing forward at a slug's pace. She got on the highway, "We go right, right?"

"Oh Jessie, I don't know!" Sarah said.

"We do, I was just messing with you."

"Very funny!" Sarah snapped back, folding her arms.

"Sorry man, bad joke." Gradually she built up speed, keeping an eye on her rearview mirror for any sign of her mom. They rode in silence for a little while.

Sarah finally broke the silence, "Why can't Frawas tell us where Joan is?"

J.R., who was nearly asleep, mumbled, "Bah-the images only fly within a three-mile radius-bah-ha of the ship, your mom said. But not with . . ." He fell into a deep slumber.

"What in the hell is he saying, Sarah?" Frawas jumped up on Jessie's lap, curled up, and went to sleep.

"He's delirious! I bet he's hallucinating."

Jessie drove on . . .

CHAPTER 55

Captured

Joan was running as fast as she could, staying low, trying to stay out of sight. The graveyard was long. She was halfway through it when the red glittering eyes appeared off in the distance. They were moving at a rapid pace, bearing in on Joan. When she saw them approaching, she dove down and crawled between two headstones. She cleared her mind and went to the place that nobody ever wants to talk about, outside the hospital ward, that is.

———

Jessie left the fog back behind them. They approached State Highway 503. She found a turnout just before they got to it. "We'll wait here. The fog stopped way back there, I think we'll be OK. Is J.R. still out?"

"Yes. I am so tired. Do you think it would be OK if we put the top up?"

"Yeah, go ahead. You can sleep up there. We'll leave J.R. where he is, and I will just snooze up here. That way if mom comes, I'll hear her and flash the lights at her. I feel comfortable here, do you?" Jessie said, now stroking the kitten on her chest.

"Yeah, but I'm really too tired to think." Sarah got up and unclasped the latch that was holding the top securely down. She raised the camper and unfolded the cot. "I'm exhausted. Wake me when your mother gets here." She climbed up, lay down, and was out.

———⁓ഏരⓄⓍⲟⲟⲱ———

Joan heard rustling around within feet of where she was hiding. She saw movement three feet away. The blood-red glowing eyes appeared to be looking directly at her. They did not move in toward her. *Whew! That was close!*

"Master, I found who caused all this turmoil! She's exactly where she needs to be! Right between these two headstones! Should I have them dig the hole or just leave her for the quaydents? After I finish her off, that is!" the ranger said with delight.

"If Featus here has his way, we would destroy her now! But now, under these new circumstances, I need her alive to finish up with the third term. She will agree or her little daughter will pay!"

Joan jumped up and sprinted between the headstones, trying to get away. It was no use, Featus was on her within two seconds. Joan never saw or even heard him coming. Featus hit her with such force that she was knocked unconscious.

The doctor screamed at Featus, "Do not hurt her! We need her intact to finish your new bride! Heather is just about used up!"

Featus stepped away with his head bowed, looking down at the ground.

The ranger went over to her, checked to make sure she was still breathing, and picked her up to carry her back to his SUV. "I'll tie her up then change my tire. I'll be over there in a half hour or so."

"Very well," the doctor said, and then turned to walk back across the field to his domicile. "Oh, one more thing. Get Jake to get everybody inside and back to routine. Then I want *him* to come talk some reason into this female! We have to move quickly, they will be sending the multitude in very soon! It will drive us elsewhere."

"Yes, Master," the ranger said as he turned to carry Joan back to the road where his vehicle was parked.

CHAPTER 56

No Joan

The sun was beating down on Jessie's face. Frawas was rubbing against Jessie's chin with her face. The whiskers tickled. Startled, Jessie sat straight up. She turned around quickly and saw J.R. sleeping on the bench seat where she had left him the night before. "*Oh man! It wasn't a dream!* Sarah?"

"Yeah?"

"It was no dream!"

Sarah looked down at J.R., then over to Jessie, "I thought not. Did your mother get here?"

"No! Let's go back up 508 and get help."

J.R. sat up swiftly. "Wait for . . . me-bah, I got to . . . pee-bah." He opened the sliding door and ran back into the trees.

"Me too!" Jessie said as she opened her door, handed the kitten to Sarah, and leaped out, running the other direction.

Sarah climbed down from the cot and closed everything up. J.R. and Jessie got back in. Jessie started up the bus. "Wait for me, I have to go too."

It was ten to fifteen minutes by the time they were on the road again. They got to the stop sign at Highway 503. "Which way do we go?"

"Not this again, Jessie! It's not funny!"

"No, I'm serious! Which way? J.R., do you know?"

"No-bah, I don't know which way . . . to go-bah. Oh . . . dear-bah, I've been trapped for way over a . . . year-bah."

"Jessie, quit messing around! I'm starting to get freaked again!"

"Seriously, I should go right, right?"

"Look Jessie, just go the way you want! I don't really care! No wait! The last time you went right and look what it got us into. This time go left."

"I don't . . . dare-bah, to . . . care-bah."

Jessie turned to the left; they went for three miles when they saw a sign. It read:

NOTROM ½ mi

Jessie hit the brakes and made her five-point turn around right in the middle of the highway. "Right on, Sarah! I have a feeling we better go the other way. What about you?"

"Yeah," Sarah agreed, looking back at J.R. He had his head in his lap, holding his face. "You'll have no argument from him, either."

They were traveling for a mile when they saw a tall, thin man carrying a duffel bag and something else tossed over his shoulder. A hitchhiker . . .

"Is that a saddle over his shoulder?" Jessie asked, as they were getting a little closer.

"It looks like it!"

"I'm not picking him up, man!" Jessie stated, as Frawas jumped on the dashboard and looked out the windshield.

"Keep on going!" Sarah confirmed.

Bam!

"*Is* that a blowout?"

CHAPTER 57

Steve?

BAM!

J.R. was sitting on the bench in the back of the bus, rocking back and forth. "Oh man, oh man, oh man," he was mumbling.

Sarah grabbed the door handle with one hand, the dashboard with the other.

Jessie swerved into the other lane briefly and then regained control. She brought the bus to a halt right after they passed the hitchhiker. "It's the driver's side front this time, so it is definitely different!"

"But it is a saddle that he's carrying! It's not Steve, though."

"Steve is dead, Sarah, of course it's not him," Jessie said, looking back at J.R. "Snap out of it, J.R! Pretend you're a man!"

J.R. sat up abruptly and said, "I can-bah, be a man! Bah-ha-ha!" Frawas jumped down off the dash and up in J.R.'s lap. She sat down and stared up in his eyes. He stared back.

Sarah and Jessie exited the bus.

"Guday ladies."

"If you change our tire, we'll give you a ride up to the next town on 503," Jessie told him.

"Sure thin, ma'am."

"The tire is bolted to the front, and the jack is just inside the back door. Put your stuff up on the luggage rack. We'll wait inside."

The girls got back into the bus. "You're such a bitch, Jessie! You didn't even ask his name. He almost looks like Steve."

171

"I don't want to know his name. I want everything to turn out differently. We're going to leave when he's finished and proceed to the next town with a cop! J.R., you sit up front with me, and Sarah you sit directly behind me. That will, in fact, change everything! You guys don't talk at all!"

They switched places. The man opened the back door to get the jack. "Is kinda hot out 'ere, ya got some water?"

"No! Just hurry so we can go!" Jessie snapped.

He closed the back and continued changing the tire.

"That was rude, Jessie!"

"Well, do you have any water?"

"No!"

"Do you want to leave?"

"Yes."

"Then shut up, Sarah!"

Sarah sat back, folded her arms over, and pouted, "He doesn't talk like him, either!" she said, under her breath.

J.R. sat there stroking the kitten, with his head resting against the dash.

The man finished changing the tire and went to Jessie's window. "Is awl finished. Whar ya want th tar?"

"Bolt it to the front and get in using the side sliding door. Thanks for changing it for us."

"No problem. My nam is—"

"Don't introduce yourself yet! I'll explain everything after we're down the road a bit."

"Your cawl," he said and then carried the tire to the front of the bus. He mounted it and got in. He looked at the trio with puzzlement in his eyes but said nothing.

They drove on . . .

CHAPTER 58

Piney Ridge

They passed the turnoff that they thought was the shortcut last time. Nobody said a word. They proceeded in silence for the next twenty minutes when finally they saw a sign that read:

PINEY RIDGE ½ MI

"Well, we're a half mile from Piney Ridge, let's see what the population is before we get excited," Jessie said, scratching her hands on the steering wheel.

Frawas jumped onto the dashboard and lay down. Sarah turned around sidesaddle in her seat to watch the signage. J.R. sat up straight and grabbed the edge of the seat with both hands. The man sitting in the back also got anxious.

The next sign read:

Population 1,123

"Do you think they'll have police in that small of a town?" Jessie asked.

"Yes, 'am, thas ware I from. Thars law n Pany Ridge. My nam is Steve."

Sarah turned around quickly, "Steve? I'm so glad you didn't tell us that earlier. You have no idea what we've just been through! If we knew your name was Steve, we would have left you way back there.

How many cops do you guys have here? Is there a restaurant? How about a phone? Do—"

Jessie interrupted, "Sarah! Stop! Steve, where is the police station?"

"Jus go up er to th lef."

"OK, thanks!"

"Ya can let me ou her. Th law got it out fer me."

Jessie pulled over as they approached the town. Steve got out, got his stuff off the rack, thanked them, and walked off toward the woods. She put it in first gear and rolled forward. J.R. went to the backseat and lay down, keeping his head lower than the window.

Sarah asked, "What are you doing, J.R? Hiding?"

"You see that . . . bar-bah? That's where we got the . . . car-bah."

"Oh shit! Did they see you?" Jessie asked sharply.

"No-bah, but the . . . guilt-bah makes me want to . . . wilt-bah-ha."

Jessie pulled up to the city hall building. "Should we all go in, or what?"

"What are we going to say, Jessie? Do you really think they'll believe us if we tell them the truth?"

"I know, I've been thinking about that too, man. What do you guys think we should do?"

"Let's go get something to eat and we'll talk about it."

"We must . . . hurry-bah, before the . . . ship-bah, will let it . . . rip-bah. Then we will really need to . . . worry-bah-ha-ha."

"What are you talking about, J.R?" Jessie asked as she put the bus in reverse.

"That is the second time you said 'ship,' what are you talking about, J.R?" Sarah questioned.

Jessie began turning to get back on the street when she noticed a man in uniform walking over to the bus. She turned back and parked back where she was. She rolled down the window. "Hi, officer. We're going to find a restaurant. Do you have any suggestions?"

"You can park here and walk across the street, or the other one is right next door. Either one has good food. What were you kids doing with Steve?"

Jessie set the emergency brake and turned the engine off. "We had a flat tire, and he helped us by changing it. So we gave him a ride. He asked us to let him out back there, so I did." Jessie opened the door and stepped out. Frawas jumped up on the dashboard and curled up.

Sarah stepped out, and as she was walking toward the officer and Jessie, she slapped the tire and asked, "Is there a gas station where we can get this tire fixed?"

"There is a station down next to the bar. You kids ought to stay away from that guy . . . Steve. He sees little green men. Not only that, but we suspect him of grand theft auto."

"Bah-ha-ha, bah-ha."

The officer looked in at J.R.

"Boy, do you want to step out of the vehicle, please? What are you kids doing so far from California?"

Jessie answered quickly, "We are taking a vacation before we go off to college. J.R. told us not to let the guy help us because he didn't trust him, but we thought he was just being overprotective as usual. I guess we were wrong. Right, Sarah?"

"Yes, and I hate it when he's right! Now he will never let us live this one down."

J.R. slid the sliding door open and exited. He walked over to them. In a very deep voice, he said, "I never trusted that man, Steve! They just don't listen. Women!" He shook his head back and forth.

Both Sarah and Jessie snapped their heads around when J.R. started talking.

The officer chuckled, "You girls best listen to him from now on. He seems to have a good head on his shoulders." He turned to walk back inside. Before the door closed behind him, he said, "You kids have a good lunch now!"

Jessie, in astonishment, asked, "Where in the hell did you get that Shawn Mullins voice?"

"Bah-ha-ha . . ."

They walked across the street. "Shit! We have no money!" Jessie said, patting her pockets.

"I have the . . . money-bah, honey. Your . . . mother-bah, treated me as . . . your brother-bah. Bah-ha-ha."

"We have to hurry!" Jessie said urgently.

"We will, Jessie. I'm going to a pay phone and calling my parents. They will send help! Before it's too late. Let's go inside and order, then I will go call."

Jessie turned to J.R., "Why can't you talk normal all the time? Although that voice is creepy coming out of you."

"Bah."

Jessie opened the door and held it for J.R. and Sarah. They went to the booth next to the window.

CHAPTER 59

Frankie

After they ordered, Sarah went to the pay phone. The answering machine picked up on the third ring. She hung up the receiver and went and plopped down at the table.

"Well?" Jessie questioned.

"It was the voice mail."

"Shit!"

"Well-bah, what the . . . hell-bah?"

"My parents let the staff off and set the voice mail when they go away. I guess they went to Europe after all," Sarah explained.

"I'll call my sister. Maybe she'll have an idea of what we should do." Jessie got up, took down Sarah's card number, and went over to the pay phone.

———— ∿∿◦⌒⊙⌒◦∿∿ ————

"Hello."

"Frankie?"

"Jessie? What's going on? I've tried to call you on Sarah's cell number, but all I got was the voice mail. Did you get any of the messages?"

"No. Frankie, listen. This really weird stuff has been happening."

"That's why I've been trying to call you. It's mom, she's gone. The hospital call . . ."

"She was here, man. Listen to what I'm say . . ."

"She's with you?"

"No! She was, but they got her!"

"Jessie! What in the hell are you doing? This is not funny!"

"I know. I'm not trying to be, man. Mom came up here to help us, and now they have her!"

"Let me talk to Sarah! You're not in the least bit amusing!"

"Do you want me to start from the beginning? It will make more sense."

"Quit playing! Mom is really missing!"

"OK, Frankie, don't talk. Just listen to what I have to tell you!"

"Go ahead."

"We came up here to Washington, we wanted to take a shortcut, and that's when everything started happening. We had a blowout."

"We, as in you and Sarah?"

"Yes! Just me and Sarah. But when we had the blowout, this guy was walking by, and he helped us change the tire."

"You didn't give him a ride, did you?"

"Yes, but that wasn't the problem. It was a good thing we did, now that I think about it. You see, we were going to camp out that night, and that's when the weirdness started."

"Get to the point, Jessie."

"I am, just listen! Me and Sarah couldn't sleep, so we went out to roast marshmallows, and we found Steve . . . dead! They got him! They ate holes in him!"

"Jessie. Put Sarah on the phone, please," Frankie said, her voice shaking.

"No! You have to listen to me. It got worse. We were trying to get back to the church, but we went the wrong way, and we found Bellowing Hollers! It's a town up here."

"Bellowing Hollers? In Washington State?"

"Yes! They kidnapped us, and that's when mom helped us escape, but they got her. She was supposed to meet us at the VW, but she never made it."

"Oh Jessie, put Sarah on, please. Is she there?" Frankie pleaded.

"Yes, she is, but she'll tell you the same thing. More than that happened, but we just need your help. We'll fill you in later. You need to sen—"

"Where are you now? Belling . . . whatever?"

"You don't believe me, do you?"

"You're talking crazy."

"I know it sounds crazy, but you have to believe me, man!"

"You're scaring me, stop messing around."

"We don't know what to do, Frankie." Jessie was wiping a tear from her cheek. "Now, we're in a town called Piney Ridge, and the cops here won't believe us if we tell them. All I know is we have to get mom out of there before they do the transplant."

"Transplant, Jessie?"

"Yes. Transplant. You really aren't believing me, are you?"

"You're really sounding like mom. Talk like that is what got her locked up, you know."

"Frankie, we really need help. Sarah's parents aren't home. They're on vacation, and we have nowhere to turn to."

"I'll help you, of course. Let me talk to Sarah, OK, Jessie?"

With a heavy sigh, Jessie said, "Hold on."

Jessie waved Sarah over. Jessie covered the mouthpiece and said, "She's not buying a word of this. She wants to talk to you." She handed the phone to Sarah and then stood there.

"Hello, Frankie?"

"Sarah, are you OK? I guess this thing that my mom has is hereditary. How long has she been having these hallucinations?"

"Frankie . . ."

"Are you all right, Sarah?"

"Yes, and so is Jessie. We'll see you soon, Frankie. Bye." Sarah, not waiting for an answer, hung up the phone.

———⌇∽∾⌇◦⌇∾∽⌇———

"She didn't believe us, did she?"

"Nope. Let's go eat and figure this thing out." Sarah turned and walked to the table.

"Shit! We're going to have to do this ourselves." Jessie followed Sarah.

CHAPTER 60

The Follow

After eating and planning, J.R. paid while Sarah and Jessie went to the ladies room. The trio met outside the restaurant. J.R. and Sarah walked down to the gas station. Jessie drove the bus down there.

"Hi, do you want me to fill it up?"

"Yeah, top it off, and I also need this tire fixed," Jessie said, getting the tire off the front end of the bus.

"It looks like it had a blowout. I don't know if I have a tire that size."

"Is there a place around here that might have one?" Jessie asked as she bolted the tire back on.

"We can order one, or you can try wrecking yards around here," the station attendant said as he finished topping off the tank.

"We're not really staying that long. The tire that is on it is new, we shouldn't have a problem."

"Suit yourself. The total is $4.87."

"Pay the man, J.R." Jessie turned back to the attendant, "Do you have a couple of gas cans I can buy?"

"Uh, sure. Come inside."

J.R. and Jessie followed the man into the shop. "We want that five-gallon one and two of the two-and-a-half gallons. Full of gas, please."

"The five-gallon one is the station's and it isn't for sale."

"Come on, we'll pay you for it. We really need it. I'll give you $25 for it."

"What do you need it for? My dad will be pissed if I sell it."

Jessie pulled the guy to the side, away from J.R. and whispered, "Our idiot friend bought a car, and he ran out of gas down the road about twenty miles back. What if we just rent the can from you and we'll bring it back?"

"How long will you have it for? I'm closing up in an hour or so."

"We're coming back here, we're going to get a room for the night. We'll bring it back in the morning."

"OK, but you have to leave a deposit."

"No problem."

The attendant filled the cans with gas. J.R. paid as Jessie strapped them to the top of the bus. They drove over to the motel.

After checking in, Frawas curled up in a ball and went to sleep on one of the pillows, while Sarah took a shower, Jessie and J.R. went to the hardware store to buy a change of clothes. After purchasing the clothing, they went to the grocery store to pick up some munchies, drinks, hygiene products, and kitten food. They went back to the room. Jessie showered next. Sarah and J.R. kicked back on the beds, not really paying attention to what was showing on the television. Jessie finished. J.R. showered last. While J.R. was in the shower, Jessie went outside. Sarah waited.

———⁓ೲ⦿⊱⦿⊰⦿ೲ⁓———

A half hour later, Jessie returned. "We've got to go!" she said as she walked through the door.

"I . . . know-bah, we must . . . go-bah. . Before the . . . day-bah, has no . . . ray-bah-ha."

"Yeah!" Jessie agreed. "We have the gas and the daylight. Let's go now, I want to be out of there before it gets dark." Frawas jumped down off the bed and clawed her way up to Jessie's arms.

"If we had a . . . gun-bah, there will be no need to . . . run-bah."

"We need a whole lot of guns, we really need help from the law. I know they won't believe us, but we can't figure out a way to get them to follow us there?" Sarah pleaded.

"If you can think of a way, let us know. We've been over all that, Sarah! We really need to hit it." Jessie swung the door open and turned to walk out. "Officer!"

"Good day again," he said.

"Officer Dungan," Jessie said, looking hard at his name tag.

"Yes, and you are Jessie Harrison?"

Frawas hissed and jumped down.

"Yes, how can I . . . how did you know?"

"I received a call from your sister. Can I talk to you and Sarah outside, please?"

"What is this about? You can talk in front of J.R."

"Jessie, please come outside with me. Sarah, you too."

Sarah got up off the bed, picked up Frawas and walked toward them. Jessie took a step out, crossed her arms, and leaned against the wall. Sarah went to the other side of the door with officer Dungan in the middle.

"Are you two girls OK? Your sister said there should only be the two of you."

"We're all right," Sarah said.

"We called my sister and were messing with her earlier. We didn't tell her about J.R. because she'll get mad. He's not holding us captive or anything."

"She asked me to keep an eye on you, Jessie, until she gets here. You can come as well, Sarah."

"What? You have no reason to take us to jail!"

Sarah cut in, "We didn't do anything. You can't take us in with no probable cause!"

"Your sister called, very concerned. She just asked me to keep an eye on you two girls until she gets here. I am not arresting you. She's just worried. That's all."

"And just how in the hell is she getting here? How long will it be? Our every intention is to leave here first thing in the morning. And that's what we're doing!" Jessie blurted out.

"That is fine with me. She'll be here by then. You have her real scared, she's flying into Seattle and renting a car to get here. She will be here first thing in the morning. Jessie, she said she is concerned about your health."

"Well, don't concern yourself!"

"By the way, why do you have the gas cans on top of your vehicle?"

"We don't want to run out of gas!" Jessie snapped.

"Oh, I see. Well, Tom, the guy that sold you the gas and rented you the gas can . . . says something a little different."

"It's none of your business!" Jessie snapped.

"Officer Dungan, it really is none of your business. We don't have to answer to you or the gas station attendant. My father is an attorney and living with him all my life has given me some knowledge of the law. You can't harass us like this for any reason. Now, if you will excuse us, we're going inside!" Sarah turned and walked in, "Are you coming, Jessie?"

Jessie turned, followed and closed the door in the officer's face. When they reentered the room, J.R. was gone. He had exited through the back window.

"Shit!" said Sarah.

The girls heard through the door, "I'll be keeping an eye on you two. I promised your sister."

Jessie yelled back at the door, "That's fine with us! Keep on watching!"

"Where did J.R. go?" Sarah whispered, putting the kitten on the bed.

"Hell if I know." Jessie went to the window and began looking around for J.R.

"This isn't working! Let's go tell Officer Dungan everything. Maybe he'll help us," Sarah said, bouncing down on the bed.

"Or throw us in the looney bin!" Jessie snapped back as she finished putting the screen back in place on the window sill. She closed the window.

"Yeah, I know you're right. I don't really want to go without J.R., but we need to go get your mom."

"Let's just drive right out of town. If they follow, great! Maybe they'll follow all the way to that hellhole. They'll see for themselves what's going on."

"The only thing I see wrong with that is if they tag along and we go get that car, then we will be arrested for grand theft auto."

"We won't stop for that car then. We'll just keep on going and drive right to town. When we stop there we'll tell them what's up. We know the general direction where they held us prisoner. The cops will have to be able to tell there is something wrong with that place." Jessie was pacing back and forth.

"We should go find J.R."

"We'll drive around town, and then if we can't find him, we'll go without him."

"Jessie, what if the cop doesn't follow us all the way there? We need more manpower!"

"We'll figure it out as we go!"

Frawas jumped down off the bed and walked to the door. "Meow."

"Let's go!" Jessie said, opening the door.

Frawas ran outside and around the corner of the motel. Jessie followed. She was under one of the bushes, using it as a cat potty. Jessie turned back around and unlocked the bus. Sarah had a bag of stuff and went to the passenger's side. Jessie unlocked the door for her and waited for Frawas to come. A few minutes later, Frawas came running from the other end of the building, following was J.R.

"Well, no shit! No, I mean chicken shit!" Jessie said, laughing.

"Bah!"

Sarah crawled to the back and unlocked the sliding door. J.R. slid it open and stepped in. Frawas ran over to Jessie's door, she opened it, picked up the kitten, and got in. They rolled back out of the parking space and exited the parking lot. Driving slowly through town, still searching for Steve, they spied the officer's vehicle pulling out from between two buildings. Dungan began to follow them. Frawas jumped up on the dashboard, curled up in a ball, and slept.

CHAPTER 61

The Feds

Tracing their path back to Bellowing Hollers, in search of the hitch-hiker: Steve. The cruiser still shadowing them, Jessie, Sarah, and J.R. were getting a bit nervous. Frawas continued to sleep. They finally arrived at the turnoff. The once thought of "shortcut" through NotroM. They turned left, still following was the cop from Piney Ridge.

"Well, Sarah, it looks like you got what you asked for: a cop to follow us," Jessie said, with an anxious laugh.

"I'm still freaked, though," Sarah answered, then looking back at J.R. "I guess not as bad as him. He's totally wiggin."

Jessie looked back at him, then shook her head. "Men! Or I should say, boys!"

"We're coming up on where we left the car and motorcycle."

"Oh . . . bah, no-bah. I . . . fear-bah. It's getting . . . near-bah-ha."

"The church should be up here on the right. Should we stop?" Jessie asked.

"We're in . . . danger-bah, of the . . . ranger-bah."

"It's broad daylight, and the cop will stop if we do, I'm sure. We'll have no problems, if he's here at all. Sarah, it's up to you. Should we see what's up here?"

"Let's go . . . back-bah, before the . . . attack-bah-ha."

"I don't know, Jessie. Maybe we should just go straight to the town."

"You mean straight to hell, Sarah!"

"It's not . . . wise, to confront these . . . lies-bah."

"Don't say that, Jessie! We need to just go get your mother! Unless you want to pull over here and convince Dungan that we're not nuts."

"I need to think for a minute. I'm pulling in here for a few." Jessie turned her right signal on and exited into the parking lot of the church. She pulled over to the picnic tables and set the brake. She opened her door and got out.

The officer was parked on the other end of the parking lot next to the church. He was sitting in his car talking on the radio.

"I have to pee," Jessie walked off toward the woods.

"Me too, wait for me, Jessie." Sarah got out and ran over to Jessie.

They finished, got back to the VW where J.R. was sitting there, just rocking. Frawas was sitting on the floor, staring up at him. Dungan was out of his car, walking over to them. The girls got in quickly; Jessie started up the engine and put it in reverse. Before he reached them, Jessie put it in first and started moving forward. Dungan turned and ran back to his vehicle. They pulled out onto the highway and proceeded toward Bellowing Hollers.

"Oh shit, man!" Jessie announced, looking in her rearview mirror.

Sarah turned around, "Why does he have his lights on, now?"

"We better . . . stop-bah, for that . . . cop-bah."

"I'm going to keep on driving."

Sarah, sitting backward in her seat now, "He's pulling up next to you, Jessie."

"I have the pedal all the way down!"

They heard over the intercom, "Pull over, Jessie! The road . . ."

"Roll down your window, Jessie. I can't really hear him that well."

Jessie rolled down the window and yelled to Officer Dungan, "What?"

"The road is closed! Pull over! You need to turn around!"

Jessie stepped on the brakes. They came to a stop. The officer stopped beside them and got out of his car. Jessie laid her head on the steering wheel. J.R. slid the door open and exited and walked over to Dungan with Sarah. Frawas climbed up and sat in Jessie's lap. Jessie looked into her eyes. There were no images.

"Dammit!" Jessie said, hitting the steering wheel. Frawas then jumped up onto the dashboard and stared off in the distance, hissing.

"Just what in the hell are you kids thinking? I tried to turn you around at the church!"

"Even if we told you, you won't believe us," Sarah said, leaning on the hood of his cruiser.

Jessie turned the bus off and opened the door. Sitting sidesaddle in the seat now, she said, "What I'm thinking is my mother is being held captive in that terrifying town, man. I need to go help her! There are strange things going on there and nobody even knows it! J.R. here was stuck there for years, and now he's all messed up! Me and Sarah were held there too. Those freaks wanted to mutilate us, and they're killing everybody in that town!"

"Jessie!"

"Don't 'Jessie' me, copper! My mom is trapped there now! If it's the last thing I do, I'm going to help her!"

The officer walked to Jessie. Sarah followed closely behind. "You must listen, Jessie. There has been a disaster up ahead, and they have the road blocked. It's a Federal deal. We had . . ."

"I can't get to my mother?"

"We had no idea of what was going on until a few minutes ago, back at the church. I don't know what kind of trip you kids are on . . ."

"Screw you!" Jessie said as she faced forward in the seat and started the VW.

Dungan reached in and took the keys from the ignition. "Let's talk about this, Jessie."

Sarah stepped in front of Dungan and said, "I'll talk to her. Can you give us a few minutes, please?"

Dungan stepped back and went over to J.R.

"Sarah, we need to go and at least see for ourselves!"

"He said it was Federal. He said it was some kind of disaster. Something major must have happened if the road is closed. Maybe they have your mom in custody. Let's play it cool and ask Officer Dungan. It seems like he wants to help us."

"Yeah, right! You saw how he looked at me when I was telling him what had happened."

"Yes I did, Jessie. You have to look at how it sounds when you're talking about it. It sounds pretty much like bullshit. Don't you think? Let's just tell him your mom is there and ask if he can find out if they have her. And if they don't have her, give them a description and tell them she needs her meds."

"I don't know, man."

"We'll draw a map of where we think that prison was. OK?"

"Man, I feel like just . . ."

"Don't say it Jessie! Let's just go talk to Dungan and tell him where your mom is. Don't tell him anything, else or he'll think we're freakin' nuts."

"I already did, and he already does!"

"It's cool, though. He'll just think you're worried about your mom. Anyway, that's what I'll tell him. Because I know he's thinking we're drugged out or something like that. So just play it cool, Jessie. I'll do the talking."

"As always! I'll keep my mouth shut."

"Yeah, Jessie, as always."

Sarah walked over to Dungan. Jessie picked up Frawas and followed. J.R. was sitting, legs crossed, on the hood of the patrol car. He appeared to be in some kind of trance.

"What's wrong with this guy? Are you kids doing crack or something?"

"We are antidrug, osifer!" Jessie snapped.

"Jessie, cool out! Officer Dungan, we have a problem. Jessie's mother is in that next town. We need to go get her because she needs her medication. Jessie's sister said her mother had gotten out of the . . . hospital without being released. Is there any way you can help us get through the roadblock and get to her mom? Please."

"I was instructed to return to Piney Ridge. You kids need to come with me. From what I understand, they are investigating as to what happened in Notrom.

Jessie pleaded, "Can we at least go up to where the road is actually blocked and see if they know anything about my mom?"

"It's a classified federal investigation. That's what I know, and all I want to know. Trust me on this one. When we get back to Piney Ridge, I will check into it for you. I'm sure when they know more, they will report it."

Frawas jumped from Jessie's arms and ran off into the woods. Jessie started after her when Dungan grabbed her arm. "Hold on there, now. You're not going anywhere."

"My cat!"

"It'll be all right. Just calm yourself. Let's walk over here and sit in my car and talk. Come on, now."

Sarah went to the edge of the road and started calling, "Here, kitty, kitty. Frawas, come here, kitty, kitty."

At that moment the kitten appeared with a man chasing behind her. He was blackened with soot and grime. He was almost unrecognizable. Dungan let go of Jessie and ran to the man. Frawas climbed up to Jessie's shoulders and purred.

"Just what in the hell are you doing out in these woods, Steve?"

Out of breath, coughing, "I knee water."

"Tell, boy! Just what are you doing out there? Did you cause all this mess?"

"Na sir, I tell you what happn, dough. Is like I say days ships nes to da water, space ship. Da alins day is here. It take off dis morning and da town . . . da town is gone now day aint no mo Bellowing Hollers."

"What stories are you making up now, boy?"

"Let him talk, please!" J.R. demanded in that deep voice.

"Who in the hell . . ."

Sarah interrupted, "Please, Officer Dungan, can we hear what he has to say?"

"Go ahead whacko, talk and then you are going straight to jail!" Dungan said, still holding Steve's arm.

Huddling around Steve, they waited anxiously. "I no somtim happen when u come out form dat . . . town. Day was esplosion dis morning. I was der when it happens. I tink der no town lef. Da

189

esplosion was da take off. Days no more animal image too. I see da military come shut it up. I take off before day shut me down too. Da big house wher you were . . ."

"That's enough now, boy!"

"Officer Dungan, he knows about the house where they took us. I'm telling you, we were there! Please, sir, let him finish." Sarah begged with him.

"That's where they're probably holding my mom. We need to know! Please, officer." Jessie added to the plea.

"We can't sit here all day! Hurry with the story, boy!"

"Da house day clear dis momen. I watch from da woods. Day take lady and short boy and doctr. Aftr day gone it get burn down. I try help when I her screemn. I is too late."

"Just who was doing the screaming, boy?"

"I bet it was Heather," Sarah said, looking down at the ground.

J.R. cut in with his deep voice, "Heather, as in Bick's beautiful flower?"

"Yes."

"Maybe we need to start from the beginning," Officer Dungan said.

"We'll fill you in, but let him finish. Please. What did the lady look like that they took out of the house? Just a second, I think I have a picture in the bus." Jessie went to the bus, put Frawas on the seat, and looked in the visor. "Here it is! Is this the woman you saw?"

"I was far far when I see dem go. Dat might be her. Affer I can't help, I follow where day go, back to town."

"So you said it was a woman, a doctor, and a short boy you followed?" Officer Dungan questioned.

"Yes, but da two guy wit em."

"Richard and Jake!" Jessie burst out.

"Bah . . . they . . . thrive-bah, to stay . . . alive-bah-ha."

Officer Dungan turned swiftly around and looked at J.R., who was still sitting on the hood of his car. "What?"

"I'll keep . . . quiet-bah, to hear about this . . . riot-bah-ha."

"Just what kind of drugs are you on, boy?"

"That's how he normally talks, officer," Sarah cut in. "What happened in the town?"

"Maybe we do need to take you back up to the roadblock so you can tell them what you know."

"No ofcer Dung, I not goin to tell dem nutin. I jus tellin you."

"Where did they take my mom, Steve?"

"Das what I gunta tell you. Da tree of dem go to da lake when da two men go checkinn da town for da people, cus is day now. Da lake is where da ship is, and das why da animals is special."

Officer Dungan grabbed Steve by the arm. "You aren't making any sense now, boy. Let's go get in the car, and I'm taking you back to Piney Ridge. I will call the Feds from there. I think you just about—"

Sarah grabbed the officer's arm with both her hands, "Please, officer. If you had ever been there, you would know. We will tell you everything! We're really not crazy. It just sounds that way right now."

"You kids come along too. Jessie, pull your vehicle over to the side of the road and come with me. We'll get this all straightened out at the hall." Dungan tossed the keys to Jessie.

"I can't."

"Jessie! Don't make me arrest you, dammit!" Dungan led Steve to the backseat, opened the door, and helped him in. "J.R., come over here please."

J.R. got off the car and walked over to the officer. "This is no . . . way-bah, to earn your . . . pay-bah-ha-ha."

Dungan assisted J.R. inside, "Sarah."

Sarah walked over. "I get a phone call, and I'm calling my father!"

"That's fine, Sarah, I'm not arresting you guys, yet."

Jessie pulled her VW off to the right side; it was still half on the road. She set the brake, locked the doors, and picked up Frawas. "This is total bullshit! If anything happens to my bus—"

"Don't worry about it, Jessie. If anything was going to happen to it, it would be done by the storyteller in the backseat," Dungan said with a chuckle.

Dungan closed the back door, locking them in. He walked around to Jessie, who had just picked up her kitten. He guided her to the passenger side of his car. "Why can't I just follow you in the bus? It's my mother's VW, and I don't want it ruined."

"After we go over this back in town and everything is hunky-dory, I or somebody will give you a lift back out here to pick it up." Dungan closed the door and walked to the other side. After he made the U-turn on the narrow road, he radioed in.

"Go . . . ahead-bah, tell us the . . . dread-bah."

"Da two men go around da town and den to go da lake. Tank God I far from da town when it esplode."

"The two guys got out before the explosion?" Sarah asked.

"De was a little way from da town when de stop and look at it esplode."

"Boy, are you saying they blew the town up?" Dungan interjected.

"Not fer me to judge. I not bom espert. Dats when I run to keep up wit dem. De go to da lake . . . to da space ship."

"That's what I'm talking about now! You are always coming up with some freakish story!" Dungan blurted out.

"Da story fer trute!"

"Just ignore Officer Dung! Tell *us* your story." Jessie turned to face Steve.

Officer Dungan glared at Jessie. "You better watch that, girl! Talk like that is going to get you in trouble," he said.

"Jessie, shut up and listen!" Sarah added.

"I not keep up. Tank God agin. Da ship. It take off and burn up da truck da two in. Is gone, just like dat! Fire from da ship start da forst and evertin is gone. I run fast da uder way till I hide when da law is comin. Is bad!"

"The curse of the . . . vampire-bah, will now . . . retire-bah-ha-ha! Bah-ha-ha."

"I want everybody to shut up until we get back to Piney Ridge. You are all too far out there for me. Four atypicals in my car, what did I do to deserve this?" Dungan got on the radio and asked the person on the other end to call the other deputy in.

"Go ahead, Steve, what is he going to do? Gag us?" Jessie said, looking in to the officer's face.

"Just what's wrong with you, girl?" Dungan said, looking back at Jessie. He made the right-hand turn back onto the highway.

"We're not arrested, so we can talk and he can't hold anything against us! Go ahead, Steve," Sarah said, glaring at Dungan through his rearview mirror.

"Now, I thought you had sense, girl," Dungan said, looking back at Sarah via the rearview mirror.

"Don't be so . . . intense-bah, that she has no . . . sense-bah."

"This is one for the records!" Dungan said, rubbing his face.

"Das all I say. I come out an see you. Is bad!"

"So you don't know if my mom was put on the ship?"

"No."

"Shit!"

"Jessie, do you believe all this?" Sarah asked.

"Do you think anybody's going to believe us when or if we tell our story? Or do you think they'll put us in the mental hospital? I mean, you saw the things they did! It's all alien anyway! If you would have seen what they did to Heather, you would know!"

There was silence the rest of the way to Piney Ridge.

CHAPTER 62

The Conclusion

As instructed, there was another officer there to help Dungan with the foursome.

Officer Dungan did, in fact, call the Agency that was taking care of the *incident* in their neighboring town. "The Agency" came promptly; they took Steve *back to the site* to question him. Steve was never seen again.

After questioning Officer Dungan, the Agency realized he checked out all right. He thought the four in question were on drugs and on an unexplained trip. He later moved to Texas and became sheriff of a small town there.

J.R. had escaped before the Agency arrived. (With a little help from the girls). The Agency flooded the town of Piney Ridge and the surrounding areas with a very large search party. All of a sudden J.R. was the most wanted man in the United States. "They" *said* he was wanted in several states for numerous crimes. He was never found.

Frawas was taken from Jessie and put in a kennel in the back room. She disappeared.

After a long interrogation, Sarah and Jessie were sent back to California with the understanding that they were going to be on probation for the next year. At the end of that year they will be evaluated to see if they would be able to live without the *so-called hallucinations*. Sarah's parents got back from their vacation and were filled in on the events that happened while they were abroad. Mr. Mueller said he would follow up on this. He was silenced immediately.

Jessie got a job and lived with her sister for the next year. They moved to Northern California. They never talked about what happened up in Washington. Everytime Frankie would bring it up, Jessie would put her finger to her lips and point to her ear with her other finger. As in "They're" listening. She was off probation now; still, she waited for several months before making her move.

Sarah went off to college, as planned. She never talked to Jessie about what had happened in Bellowing Hollers. They both knew they were being watched and would be dealt with if they talked about it. She studied hard and was an honor student her first year. She too waited for the right time.

ABOUT THE AUTHOR

Dez Tovar is the self-proclaimed best author in Ferris, Texas. Being an OTR truck driver afforded her the solitude she needed to write. Driving through Terre Haute, Indiana, inspired her to write this story. She now lives on a small farm at the outskirts of Ferris with her two cats, three dogs, a steer, and seventeen chickens. She enjoys the peace and quiet of living in her country home and enjoys spending her spare time with family and friends.

CPSIA information can be obtained
at www.ICGtesting.com
Printed in the USA
FFOW05n0647251017